I0589112

What We All Quietly Scream For

A Novel

Jane Comer

ISBN-978-0-9885280-6-2

Theatredust Books
Portland, Oregon

For Debra

CHAPTER ONE

January 23, 2014

Hi, Clark. I'm really writing this to me. It's been so many years, and I have no idea of where to send this letter, and even if I did, what would be the use? If you believe I don't ever think about you anymore, you'd be very wrong. How could I not think of you? I lived with you. We married each other. As you may remember, I've always believed that once you spend some time sleeping with someone, you can never be separated from them. Not completely. Yes, Clark, I still think of you. I still dream about you. You probably think I hate you, but if you do you're very wrong. I've never known anybody else like you, and I know I never will.
Jenny Whittington Medily

Clark Jackson's Journal

January, 1982

Sometimes I still cry. It's almost been two months since I had to watch as my wife Jenny was taken away in handcuffs by the police, at my request. The image still brings out the red in my eyes. My life has been pretty loud since I graduated from high school two years ago, with things moving along very quickly. But now everything is so quiet. I go through the routines and rituals of normal living, but I don't feel alive anymore. All I have are pieces. Pieces of a broken dream. The best I can now do is try to put the pieces together and see if the dream was really ever worth having.

June 18, 1980

I took a life this day. Not a human one, but a life just the same. Months earlier, I had graduated from high school. I tried going to a local teachers college, but found it boring, and quit. I didn't have a clue what to do now. My parents made the not so quiet suggestion that I find something to fill my idle hours with, preferably a job of some kind. That's why I was driving down the country highway that led from my parents' home. A new hamburger place in Salem was looking for people, and I wanted to be one of them. Jobs weren't easy to come by in this part of the world. The day before, I had waited in line with two hundred others. My hope was to get one of five jobs open at another restaurant, but I had not succeeded. This hamburger place was new, however, and needed a whole new crew. Taking no chances this time, I decided to wear my graduation suit from high school. I needed any edge I could get.

My single speaker AM radio was blasting out disco music as I raced my gold Volkswagen Bug around the curves I thought I knew well. Even if I had been paying more attention, I'm sure there wasn't any way I could have avoided hitting the deer standing in the middle of the road as I spun around a corner. I swerved sharply to the left, but so did the deer. The tan deer went spinning back to the center of the road after hitting my right fender. With arms and legs shaking, I crawled out of

my car. I watched as the animal strug-
gled to stand on her hopelessly broken
legs. Her sad eyes met mine, and I felt
as if I should do something, like say a
prayer, maybe. But I didn't have any
memorized prayers handy. Before I
could make something up, I saw a man
coming my way who looked as if he
might know what to do. "Thank God,"
I said, and left my prayer at that.

"Yeah," the man said after reaching
the scene of the crime. "I thought I
heard the sounds of another poor, de-
fenseless creature of the wild getting it.
I don't know why people insist on driving their cars like they're in some kind
of drag race." Grabbing the deer by its
hind legs, he pulled it over to the side
of the road.

"Didn't that just give that poor, de-
fenseless creature even more pain?" I
asked.

"Naw. She can't feel a thing now
that she's dead."

"She's dead already?"

"Sure. The shock alone killed her."
The man looked carefully at the deer.
"Yep. This is the doe who gave birth a
few days ago. What a shame." For the
first time, he looked over at me. "You
okay?"

"Yes, At least I think I am."

"You look healthy enough," he said, sounding disappointed. "Have you looked at your car yet? No telling how much damage an accident such as this might have done to a thin metal German car." This made the man seem happier.

The words "accident," and especially "damage," echoed inside my brain as we walked over to my car. I looked at the right fender, and quickly wished I hadn't. Little was left of it. What once was shiny gold painted metal was now a flattened collection of pleated ripples. The headlight wasn't broken, but the plastic chrome colored rim around it was. I just wanted to leave. "Do you think it would be okay if I took off?"

"Sure. Go ahead. I'm used to cleaning up after things like this. Just don't forget to file an accident report with the State. "

Still shaking, I climbed back into my bruised Bug. The memory of hitting the deer kept returning. I, however, refused to let it make me feel guilty. After all, the deer was dead, and there wasn't anything I could do to change that.

But I was still very much alive, and in need of a job. Still, it wasn't until I reached Salem that I realized I hadn't turned off my emergency blinkers.

Rod's Hamburgers was a small chain of restaurants owned by a man named Rod Casum. Other than that, all I knew about them was two things. One was that they were a lot like McDonald's. The other was that they were known in Oregon for their slogan, which encouraged people to "aim for Rods." In keeping with this slogan, every Rod's outlet featured a large neon sign shaped like a revolver. I didn't know if I wanted to work for a place like this, but my resume was a bit skimpy. Other than chores for my father, I hadn't worked anywhere yet.

Upon entering Salem, I took the West Salem exit. West Salem was a quaint combination of industrial and residential districts on the West side of the Willamette River. Then panic hit me. I had assumed all I had to do was find the revolver sign, but there wasn't one to be seen. Finally, on my fourth trip up the street where it was supposed to be located, I noticed a large cardboard sign on a mostly constructed building. The sign read "apply here." Braking the Bug, I ran inside, not sure if this place was Rod's, or some other burger joint. It didn't really matter anymore.

It was Rod's. And it was also a den of pure chaos.

Workmen were still at work on finishing the interior, and doing so required using equipment louder than a Rock guitar.

The seating area wasn't the sort one expected to find at a fast-food joint. The place was actually attractive. It had rich brown plastic cushions on the seats. The walls featured genuine synthetic walnut paneling. The tinted windows displayed well the charming homes that smiled down from the West Salem foothills. There, right in the middle of the dining room, was something I'd never seen in a fast-food joint before. A fireplace. A gas fireplace, oval in shape, made of tan bricks.

The multitudes of fellow applicants were gathered around the fireplace, like cattle. However, I've never seen cattle so eager for the branding iron. This, however, didn't stop me from joining the herd. I filled out an application, then went and got in line behind what seemed to be two-hundred people. But the line wasn't moving. "Aren't they doing interviews yet?" I asked the girl in front of me.

"They're not doing interviews," the girl said. "I guess the manager has another way of hiring people."

"Oh," I said. "What is it?"

"He didn't say anything, except to stand here in line."

I stood there, eyeing my competition. They seemed to know each other, perhaps because they all went to school together. Then my eyes connected with those of a girl who, like me, didn't seem to know anybody. She was blond, blue eyed, and tiny. I don't know what it was about her that I found interesting, except perhaps the curious sense of sadness that came from her eyes. The girl and I spent a few seconds looking at each other, as if some sort of bond already existed between us. I didn't even know her name, but I already felt as if I'd known her since time began. Before I could even wave at her, a man emerged from the kitchen area, and locked the door so no one else could come in and apply.

"Is everyone here done filling out your applications?" he asked loudly. All but a couple of people said yes. "You two can finish later. Just take your place in line for now. My name is Jay Leiber." He made a face as a workman started using a loud power tool, and waited until the noise ceased. "I'll be managing this restaurant. Now, I want everyone to count off in fours. Just as in PE class."

Some of the kids looked at each other strangely, but count off we did. "Three," I said, trying to sound confident.

"Okay," Jay said when we were finished counting. "I want all the three's to go stand over there." I, and all the other three's walked to the corner of the dining room Jay had pointed to. Jay walked back to the door, and unlocked it. "I want the rest of you, the one's, two's, and the four's, to go home now."

"Where should we leave our applications?" asked one girl.

"Put them in the garbage on your way out."

"What?"

"These people are hired," he said, pointing to the three's. "You folks are all out of luck." Amid much grumbling, the kids all trashed their applications on the way out. One guy walked up to Jay and tore up his application in front of him, allowing the pieces to fall on the tile floor. When the last of the losers finally had left, Jay calmly turned back to us. "Now, please give me your applications on your way out, and I'll be calling you each to arrange your training." We marched like good soldiers up to him, handing him our applications. Just ahead of me, I saw the pretty little blond girl. But she disappeared out the door before I could give Jay my application. After giving him my info sheet, I raced out the door, but she had vanished. Oh well, I thought, as I got into my Bug. I'll get to know her better very soon. As I drove home, neither hitting the deer, nor my smashed fender mattered. Because I now had a job. I was a SUCCESS.

Jenny's Diary

Got a job at a burger place today. Mom said I needed to earn my keep. Lucky jobs are easier to find here in Salem than they were in Longview. I guess I'm lucky. I really don't want to work. Saw a guy at the interviews who was tall and good looking. I can't believe he showed up to apply for work at a burger place wearing a suit! He got hired too. So I guess I'm going to hold off on getting fired from this job. I think we would make really good looking babies together.

CHAPTER TWO

Clark Jackson's Journal

When I arrived home, my father examined my damaged fender. "You young guys sure know how to wreck cars," my father said, laughing. "I've told you about the time I totaled my 58 Mercury, haven't I?"

"Yeah," I answered. "And how both you and the car skidded upside down through two intersections." "The car got crushed, but I didn't have a mark on me!"

"When should we call the insurance company?"

"That won't be necessary," he said, taking a moment to examine the damage more closely. "No, a little accident like this costs much more when the insurance people pay for it."

"Why's that?"

"Because, the next time the premium comes due they'll jack up the rates. We should be able to fix this easily ourselves. Only four bolts hold these Vee Wee fenders on, if I remember right."

"Where can we get a new fender?"

"Any junkyard. Find one, and we'll get together and spend a few minutes sticking it on. Then you can get someone to paint it the right color."

Soon Dad was on his way back to the office. He not only worked for IBM, often he worked for them morning, noon, and night.

June 20, 1980

"Mistake," Darrel Hankman said, between sips of orange pop.

"But Darrel, I've got to work somewhere" I insisted.

Darrel was my best friend, though I often wondered why. He was critical of everything, and had an annoying habit of speaking in one word sentences. He was my friend, though, so I was hanging out with him as he worked the night shift at a convenience store, trying to save money for his fall college plans.

"College." Darrel said.

"I don't want to go to college just yet," I said.

"Why?"

"I've been in school all of my life. I want to a break for a while." I swilled a mouthful of my cola.

"Ridiculous," Darrel grumbled, shaking his head with total disgust. Just then a guy with a bag of corn chips headed for the door. "PAY!" Darrel shouted. Trembling, the guy came back and paid.

June 21, 1980

Nervously preparing for my first day of work, I got out of bed too early, showered too quickly, and left with too much time to spare. Jay had called to tell me that because I lacked experience, he was sending me to train at another Rod's. I arrived in Salem a half hour ahead of schedule. Thinking they'd consider me a jerk for showing up early, I parked half a block away for twenty minutes before finally finishing my trip. I experienced the new sensation of walking through a door marked "employees only," and once inside I stood watching the busy kitchen area.

This place was much older and larger than the place I had applied at.

"Shannon, someone's here," shouted a uniformed girl, making me feel like a trespasser.

"And what can I do for you?" a short, blond woman asked.

"I'm Clark Jackson, and Jay Leiber said I was to report here for training."

Now that she knew I wasn't someone she had to be nice to, the half smile on the woman's face dissolved into a frown. I heard a disembodied voice call out from behind the grill. "Shannon, is that another one?"

"Yes," said the woman, as if I wasn't there. "And the next time I see Jay, I'm going to read him the riot act. I don't see how he thinks we can just drop everything to train these idiots he hired right off the sidewalk!"

"I'm sorry," I said.

The woman looked at me sternly. "It's not your fault you're the second untrained idiot who has walked in here today. It's also not your fault that I didn't know about either of you. Breaking in one new person makes my head throb. Two makes it explode, so watch your step. Have you ever worked in a restaurant before?"

I looked at her, and wanted to run out the door. "No," I said softly. "This is the first job I've ever had."

She slapped her forehead with disgust, before talking to me as if I were an infant. "Well, first you need to punch in on the time clock. You do know how to punch in on a time clock, don't you?"

She gave me a hard stare with her green eyes, and all I could do was shrug an embarrassed no. Grabbing me by the arm, she led me to the clock and taught me how to use it, and use it well. Then she took me to a small room she called the employee's lounge. This dark little closet of a room stored forty or so tanks containing soft drink syrup. This left only enough room for one small table. At that table sat the blond girl with sad blue eyes I had noticed at the hiring session. The girl and I spent a few seconds looking at each other. I didn't even know her name, but felt as if I had known her all my life. She was the girl of both my day and night dreams. She had her blues eyes, and her curly yellow blond hair draped her head like that of a doll's. Her lips shyly turned in. Her chin slightly turned downward, not enough to be receding, but just enough to add to her overall delicate appearance. She was the very image of the girl I'd always wanted.

"This is Jenny," Shannon said, snapping me out of my daydream. "You two will train together." She handed both of us a pamphlet. "These manuals tell the essentials of what you need to know to work at Rod's. Of course, there's no substitute for experience."

Shannon left us alone, and we quietly studied the manuals. Sometimes Jenny would catch me peeking at her. She would smile shyly, and we would both return to reading. Finally, I looked up to catch her peeking at me.

"Have you ever worked in a place like this before?" I asked, after inhaling deeply.

"I worked at a McDonalds once," she said, in a voice barely above a whisper.

"Well, that's pretty close to a Rod's," I said. She smiled, but went back to reading.

I didn't learn much from the manual, distracted as I was by Jenny. It also didn't help that the book was at least fifteen years old, and full of instructions such as how much hair spray the girls could use on their hair.

Finally, Shannon let us go to work. All she let us do that first day was make drinks for the orders the experienced workers took.

The week continued. Gradually Shannon let us do more and more. Having been a haphazard ham most of my life, I found being a fast-food counter boy very easy. Jenny, however, was having a hard time overcoming her shyness. As the days went by, I tried my best to break through her layer of shyness. Finally, one day, after we punched out together, I made my first big move.

She was sitting at one of the plastic lobby tables as I approached. "Hi, Jenny," I said.

"Hello, Clark," she said softly.

"Are you waiting for someone?"

"Only the bus."

"Well," I said, feeling like a smooth operator. "I've got my car outside. How about a ride home?"

She looked a little scared. "I live in West Salem."

"That's perfect. It's on the way."

Jenny's eyes grew happy as she realized she didn't have to take the bus.

After what seemed like an entire ice age, she gave her answer. "Okay." She rose from the table, started to walk out with me, but stopped. "I forgot my watch," she said, feeling her bare wrist. "I forgot to put it back on after washing the dishes."

"I'll go get it."

"Would you? It's blue."

Running into the kitchen, I located the timepiece, which Jenny had left among the plastic dishes. These were the dishes the employees had to use instead of the wax and paper products the customers got. I quickly ran back out to the lobby, but Jenny was nowhere to be seen. Looking out the window, I saw a bus pulling away from the curb. And in one of the window seats I could see the back of Jenny's curly blond hair. Staring at the watch in my hand, I decided not to stick it in Shannon's lost and found box. Instead, I would hang onto it and give it to Jenny myself the next day. Walking out to my car, I grew even gloomier as I saw that the tire underneath the crushed fender had gone flat. As I got out my jack and my spare, I tried not to scream. I kicked the flat tire instead.

CHAPTER THREE

June 25, 1980

Some days destined to be disasters, and for me this has to rank in the bleak top ten of my life. Staying home and washing my underwear would have been more productive than going to work turned out to be. I would prefer not to discuss this day at all, but if this story is to continue I suppose I must.

First, I should never have looked out the window. Then I wouldn't have discovered that the blue skies of yesterday had decided to wear murky gray overcoats today. This alone made me feel like staying home, but all I had to do was think of Jenny, and I was out the door.

Sure, she had ducked out on me the day before. Despite that, I couldn't my fantasies of what life would be like with

Jenny. Why, today just might be the day that we look into each other's eyes and dance into romantic heaven. Or at the very least, she might say hi.

After just three days of working at Rod's Hamburgers, the work was becoming boring. However, I always know how to make my world interesting. I was almost late. As I rushed into the kitchen area, I ran into Jenny. Literally. She was carrying several cabbage heads that were to become coleslaw. I wanted to help her chase the cabbage heads, which were bouncing away like rubber balls, but Shannon called me in to her office.

"Now, if you'd been here on time, you would already know," she said.

"Know what?"

"Today's your last day here. The West Salem location opens next week."

"That quickly? I thought it would take longer."

"Jay Leiber has decided he wants to open early. He feels he needs to work some of the bugs out of you bozos before the grand opening. And both you and Jenny are getting off early today, because Jay is having an employee meeting at the new place."

"Is the meeting here?"

"No, of course not. If you had any IQ. Anyway, it's at the new place. For right now, though, I want you to go out there and work hard; you know, like you care. If I were Jay, you'd already disappeared." Shannon slid out of her chair, and left me there to nurse my charred insides.

My shortened shift went smoothly. Shannon let both Jenny and me off at one, which left two hours before the three o'clock meeting. "Here's your watch," I said to my dream girl, as we were punching out.

"I'm sorry I left yesterday," Jenny said, looking embarrassed. "I walked out to your car, and saw that you had a flat. Then the bus pulled up, and I didn't want to miss it."

"Oh," I said, relieved. I raised my courage and offered Jenny a ride. I expected her to say no, but she nodded her head yes. I nervously led her out to the Volkswagen. Since there was a couple of hours before the meeting, Jenny wanted to go home first. The trip to her place occurred without mishap. Of course, nothing wonderful happened, either. She just sat and said very little. When we arrived at her mom's apartment, I asked if I could stay and visit.

Surprisingly, she said sure. The most wonderful "sure" I've ever heard uttered. She asked if I minded waiting in her living room while she changed out of her work clothes.

"Sure," I said.

We entered a clean, tidy living room, full of well-used furniture. Doilies covered every flat surface. In one corner stood an upright electric organ, with piles of Gospel music resting on top of it. In the opposite corner was an old army footlocker with a color television sitting on top. The set was on, tuned to a popular soap opera. Directly across from the TV, stretched across a couch, slept a human being.

"That's my Mom," Jenny explained. "She drove all the way back from Tacoma early this morning." I felt uneasy. I couldn't recall a single movie or TV show where someone met his potential girlfriend's mother this way. "You wait here while I go change," Jenny said. She left me there, looking down at her mother's sleeping face. At least she isn't snoring, I thought. She was middle aged, with red hair and a pleasant face. Her red hair made me pause to consider whose hair, mother's or daughter's, was real, since Jenny's was golden blonde like mine. I concluded that Jenny must get her color from her father. Suddenly, the woman became conscious.

"Who are you?" the woman asked, with a sleepy, startled tone.

Hovering over the woman, embarrassment kept me from speaking. Just when everything was getting sticky, though,

Jenny returned to make introductions, and all was cool. Just the same, however, Jenny and I quickly made our escape to the overcast surroundings outside.

Scraping our feet along the asphalt, we walked in a circular direction around the parking lot of her apartment building. For the longest time we said very little, just listening to the sound of our feet. We would glance at each other, and as quickly look away again. It thrilled me anyway. As for Jenny, I could only hope she was too, though I couldn't be sure. A key trait of Jenny was her quietness, and it surprised me when she began what for her was a lengthy discourse.

"I sure do like this part of town," she said. "I've only been in Salem a few months, but it sure beats Longview."

"Longview, Washington?"

"Yes, that was my hometown for a while. Only I can't go back there any-more...". She stopped, as if she were revealing an awful secret. Her pupils grew small, and she became her quiet self again.

"Well, what are some of your hobbies?" I thought it was a good idea to try to change the subject.

She stopped walking and leaned up against a tree. She sweetly looked up at me with her blue eyes. I had the feeling she was trying to devise something that would please me. She finally smiled before saying "I write some."

This brought me joy. "That's great. I write too. What do you write about?"

"Oh, just poems and junk."

"What are they about?"

"Things."

"What sort of things?" I asked, with mock impatience.

"Nothing. Nothing at all," she answered playfully.

"Do you write a lot?"

"Enough to fill a whole book."

"Do you ever think about getting any of it published?"

"No, I couldn't. I mean, I could never let anyone else read it." Sounding embarrassed, Jenny turned away.

"But you haven't really written something until you allow someone to read it." I froze after saying this, hoping I hadn't made Jenny angry.

Jenny took it well. "Well, I guess I'll have to let you read it sometime," she said, smiling.

This made me feel brave. "Jenny, I think you're really cute," I said abruptly.

Jenny lowered her chin into her chest like an embarrassed little girl and said softly"okay."

Though we continued walking for a while longer, little communication took place. We made small talk, looking at each other with fleeting glances.

I drove her the short distance to the new, finished restaurant. Sitting at a table, watching our new coworkers drift in, we began communicating again.

"Do you have any brothers or sisters?" I asked.

"There's eight of us. Six girls, two boys."

"Whoa. Must have been tough to take a shower," I laughed. Jenny looked grim. "Do your folks believe in big families?"

"No. They just wanted two boys, and kept trying until they had them."

"They must have been happy when they finally got what they wanted."

"No. They got a divorce when I was twelve. Now they hate each other's guts." Tears came to Jenny's eyes. For me, nothing worse in the universe could have occurred. I had made Jenny cry.

"I think what your parents did is simply awful," I said, trying to redeem myself "When people make a commitment such as marriage and children, they should keep it, no matter what. Nothing's as important as family."

Jenny's expression changed from dour to ecstatic, and she gave the brightest smile I have yet seen. Before we could communicate more, the meeting began.

"In case some of you can't remember," Jay said, "my name is Jay Leiber, and I'll be the maestro of this orchestra."

A kid in the back raised her hand. "I thought this was a restaurant," she said. When everyone laughed, she did too, though we could all tell she didn't know why.

"Well," Jay said, "on this note let's get started. Allow me to introduce Denna Scaper, our assistant manager. She'll be in charge of personal appearance. Denna?"

Jay sat quickly, and Denna slowly made her way from the center of her chair to the center of attention. Every inch of her five foot three frame was trembling. She looked over at Jay, who gave her a nod of encouragement. She then focused her eyes at her feet as she spoke.

"Long hair," she said, "what I mean is, you gals with long hair will have to keep it pulled back. Also... out of the eyes?" She looked back at Jay, who nodded his head. "Guys, too. You all look okay now. But let your hair grow, and you'll have to do what the girls do....". She looked back at Jay again." Fingernails, right?" she asked. Jay nodded. "Fingernails." She stopped, looking as if her mind had been erased. Fear brought moisture to her eyes, and Denna suddenly turned and ran to the rest rooms.

"Well, that's Denna," Jay said, standing again. Jay took over, telling us about our need for cleanliness and a professional appearance.

At the end of the meeting, Denna reappeared to help give out the baseball hats and red stripped T-shirts that were to be our uniforms. I went to Jay to get mine, while Jenny approached Denna. However, when I finished helping Jay find an extra large for me to wear, I saw Jenny walking out the door.

"See you tomorrow, Clark," Jay shouted as I exited through the back door. The overcast skies had turned liquid, rain was pouring down. I saw Jenny, waiting to cross the street, and ran to her.

"I thought you were going to wait for me, Jenny," I said as struggling to regain my breath.

"No. I want to go home now," Jenny replied, her hair as wet as spaghetti.

"I'm all finished. Let me drive you home."

"Good-bye," Jenny said, running across the street. I stood and watched until she disappeared, wondering what I had done wrong.

Jenny's Diary

Guess I'd better write some more in this. I told Clark that I'd written a whole book's worth of stuff. Sometimes I can be such a liar. It's just that he's so smart, and I don't want him catching on to how stupid I am. I have to get together with him. I don't have many other options. I so want to get on with my life. Mom already had her first baby by the time she was my age.

CHAPTER FOUR

Clark Jackson's Journal

July 5, 1980

The fog of the grease burned as it drifted into my eyes.

Still, I couldn't let this slow me down. I had enough meat on the grill for thirty hamburgers. Worse, I didn't know what I was doing. It figured. Just when I was getting used to being a counter boy, Jay took me aside and announced I was now a grill person. "Since it's the middle of the afternoon, business should be dead," Jay had said before rushing out the door to the bank. However, I was the one who turned out to be dead. As soon as Jay left, half of West Salem walked in, all wanting fresh hot hamburgers. The two girls in front had little trouble punching up the orders and calling them back to me as if they were both auctioneers. I, in a panic, mumbled the orders back, but forgot them as soon as I said them. I put plenty of meat patties on the grill, but forgot about putting fries in the fryers, and wasn't even thinking about preparing the buns. Then Jay came rushing back in, horror scribbled all over his face.

"What do we need?" he screamed.

"I don't know."

"You what?"

"I'm not used to this...".

Jay looked at me as if I were something he had just stepped in. Then in mere minutes, he filled the orders. "It's obvious you have a way to go on the grill," he snarled, after things had returned to a normal dullness. He then sent me out to collect all the garbage scattered along the nearby street.

As the days went by, I continued trying to find some way to prove to Jenny how sincere my feelings were. Every chance I had, I tried to talk with her at work, but it usually went the way this conversation in late July did. "How you doing, stranger?" I asked, since it had been several days since I'd worked with her.

"Fine," Jenny mumbled.

"Have you been enjoying the weather?"

"Jay, he's bugging me," Jenny said, though in a voice only loud enough for me to hear. I got the point, and stayed quiet the rest of that day.

Many other days I tried to start conversations with Jenny. Most of them turned out like the previous example. There were, however, moments when she would be friendlier, and even lightly joke with me. Of course, I wouldn't have continued being such a pest if I wasn't sure Jenny secretly cared about me.

It wasn't long before I decided to try sending her a love note. On the day I thought of it, I was working a day shift. Jenny wasn't working until the evening. As soon as I finished my shift, I raced to the grocery store across the street and bought her a card. It had a picture of a sunset on the outside, and the inside was blank. Returning to Rod's, I sat in the lobby. I composed the note to Jenny, while she was working only a few feet away:

Dear Jenny,

I'm sorry for bothering you. I just want you to know I care a great 'deal about you, and want to be your friend. I know you haven't lived here long, and you don't know who to trust. Let me tell you there's not a single person in this town who would want to hurt you. You are too sweet for that. You are a wonderful girl, and I would make a big mistake if I didn't become your friend.
Love Clark.

I slid the card into an envelope and wrote Jenny's name on the outside, adding the best flower I'd ever drawn. I sneaked back to the employee's lockers, slid the card into Jenny's, and waltzed out the door.

Walking into work the next morning, I could see that Jenny had liked the note simply by the look on Denna's face.

"Oh, Clark," she said, "that card was so beautiful."

"So Jenny got it?" I asked, worried that maybe I had slid it into Denna's locker accidentally.

"Did she? I've never seen a girl look so happy. I told her it was obvious how much you care about her."

"Do you think she likes me?"

"After that card, she'd better."

An hour had to pass before Jenny reported to work. I was standing near the back door chopping lettuce when my dream girl arrived, exactly two minutes and thirty-six seconds before her shift began. Upon seeing me, her face exploded into a smile, and she said "hi." It was the best "hi" I had ever heard. She went to put on her apron and punch in, and didn't say anything more to me. Every so often, though, she would look my way and smile.

I wanted to talk with Jenny, but it didn't seem possible.

I had to be there all day, and she was working a short shift. However, moments after telling Jenny she could go home, Jay let me take my ten minute break. He added that if I were fast enough, I might catch Jenny before she left. Tearing off my apron, I ran out to the lobby, the direction I'd seen Jenny go. I wasn't fast enough, though. Jenny wasn't to be seen. I stared out the window in the direction of her apartment complex, but couldn't see her. A day that I had started with great hope was now lousy, and I slumped into a booth, tears building in my eyes. Then I saw a plastic bag land directly in front of my eyes. "Clark, could you watch my stuff while I go to the girls' room?" Jenny asked. "I need to brush out my hair."

"Sure," I said, trying but failing to look to look calm. When Jenny returned, it was with lightness in her movements, and sweetness in her face. For the first time in ages, she relaxed around me. Without us saying anything, there was something special between us. I knew it had to be the special bond that has always existed between a man and a woman in love.

"I really liked the note, Clark," my dream girl said.

"Nobody's ever done something that grand for me before."

"I hoped you would like it," I said. "But that can't be the first time a guy's put a note in your locker." My heart was beating so fast I was sure Jenny could see it moving in and out of my chest.

"Did you mean it when you said you wanted to be friends?"

"Yes."

"Well, I wouldn't mind being friends with you," she said, emphasizing the word friends.

Of course, I wanted to be more than just friends with her. I figured, though, that it was still an improvement over the way things had been between us. "What have you got planned for the rest of the afternoon, my friend?" I asked, starting to feel more relaxed.

Jenny smiled when I called her my friend. "I was going shopping downtown," she said.

"Shopping for what?"

"I want to get myself a cowboy hat," she said.

"I'm stuck here all afternoon. If I wasn't, I'd ask to go with you."

"I wish you could. Maybe I could stop off here on my way back to show you what I look like in my new hat."

"I'd love that." I looked up at the clock, and saw that it was already time for me to go back to work. Jenny saw the time, too, but neither of us did anything about it, talking a while longer.

"Do you still live just up the street?"

"Not for long. My Mom and step dad are moving back to Arizona soon. That's all they do, is move back and forth from Arizona to Oregon, and vice versa."

"Why?"

"You got me."

"Are you going with them?" I asked nervously.

"I always have. But this time I'd rather get my own place and go on living here. I don't like Arizona. It's too hot."

"I don't want you to go either, Jenny. Why, I'd marry you to keep you from going away!"

Jenny looked straight into my eyes, a stunned, scared look on her small, delicate face. "Well, anyway," she said, not commenting on what I'd said. "I hope I get to stay here because I really like Salem. I'm really tired of always moving around." She looked up at the clock. "You'd better get back to work."

"Okay," I said. "But be sure to come back and let me see you in your new cowboy hat."

"I'll try," she said, standing and grabbing her plastic sack. Just that quickly, she was out the door.

I was in a numb state for several seconds. Then I noticed I was five minutes late returning to work. I scurried back to the grill, putting on my apron as I went.

"How'd it go?" Jay asked.

"Not bad. She wants to be friends with me."

"That's a start," Jay said. He reached into his pocket, and handed me a toothbrush. "Now, I want you to get started scrubbing the back floor."

"With a toothbrush? Why?"

"Five minutes late from break is why."

"Oh." I glumly started scrubbing the floor, figuring it was a fair price to pay for five extra minutes with Jenny. After a half hour, Jay gave me a regular push broom, much to my tired hand's relief.

Jenny didn't stop by while I was still on the job. When my shift was over, I sat in the lobby in case she still might come by. Finally, I walked outside and drove off in my VW. But this still had been a great day. Jenny had talked with me, had said she wanted to be friends with me. I couldn't sleep that night. I was too happy to sleep.

CHAPTER FIVE

I didn't see Jenny again for a couple of days. I managed to be at the restaurant the next day she was scheduled to work, though it was my day off. Jenny didn't show up. In a panic I sought out Jay. "Did Jenny say anything about being late today?" I asked.

"Why do you want to know?" Jay asked calmly. "Is this girl important to you, or something?"

"Jay, come on."

"Sure. She said she would be a few minutes late. She's moving into her own place. Maybe you should see if she wants a roommate."

Ignoring Jay, I went out to the lobby and waited. When Jenny finally appeared, she didn't notice me.

After punching in, Jay sent her back to wash a sink full of dishes. Aiming to be subtle, I crept up behind her. "Hi,

Jenny," I said, trying to recreate the lightness of our last meeting. "How have you been doing?"

"Fine," my dream girl said, not looking away from the dishes.

"I hear you've got your own place now." "Yes."

"I was thinking maybe I could come over for a visit sometime." I looked at Jenny for some sort of response, but she gave none. "What do you say?"

"I really don't feel like getting together with you right now," she said, with no particular emotion.

"Oh, okay," I said, in a voice that contained every emotion there is. "But..., but when you do feel like getting together..., just let me know."

"Okay," Jenny said, still not looking up from the dishes. I left the restaurant all confused. I didn't understand why Jenny had suddenly closed herself off from me. If only I could get her to see how honest, pure, and total my love was for her, it would be impossible for her not to love me, too.

Half a week passed before my next opportunity with Jenny came. Jay had begun letting me run the restaurant Sunday nights. It made me feel important, though we didn't have much business Sunday nights. Jenny didn't work on Sunday nights. But on this Sunday night she was on call, and when one of the two regular girls called in sick, there she was working under me on my shift. I couldn't believe my luck. Midway through the night, as usually was the case Sundays, we ran out of work, and were all standing around.

Cathy, the other girl working this night, asked if I thought we'd get out as soon as we closed. "I think that's a safe bet," I said, gesturing toward the empty dining room. "But we'll have to work as a team," I added, trying to sound managerial.

"I hear you've got your own place now, Jenny," Cathy said to Jenny. "That must be really cool."

"It's grand," Jenny said softly.

Cathy moved her auburn brown eyes back and forth at Jenny and me, and I knew she could see there was tension between Jenny and me. "Clark, would be okay if I ran to the girl's room to adjust my hair? It's really difficult to get it to stay under this baseball hat."

"Sure. It doesn't look like any customers will be coming in here the next few minutes." When Cathy left, I worked up my courage before speaking to Jenny. "I thought you wanted to be friends," I said.

"What?" Jenny asked, looking scared to death. "I said I thought you wanted to friends."

"I am your friend, Clark."

"Well, you don't show it very well."

"I'm sorry," Jenny said, suddenly looking as if she were going to cry.

The last thing I wanted was for Jenny to cry. "I'm sorry, too. I didn't mean to be mean." Jenny turned away and began nervously cleaning the counter with a bar towel. I stared down at the empty grill.

Then Cathy returned from the restroom. "Jenny," Cathy said, "you never did finish telling me about living on own. Is it as fabulous as it sounds?"

"Oh, sure," Jenny said, still sounding sad.

"Clark," Cathy said, "do you have your own place too?" "No. I'd like to, though," I said. I hadn't really thought about it, but in my love for Jenny I would say just about anything.

"Well," Cathy said. "Jenny only works half as many hours as you do, and she can afford her own place. You should too."

"True," I said.

"There's an apartment available in my complex," Jenny suddenly said.

"There is?" I said, almost gulping at the thought Jenny would suggest what she was suggesting.

"Yeah," Jenny continued. "They don't cost much, and they're not that bad if you don't mind a few spiders and that you'll be living straight across from me."

"I'll have to check into it," I said. I tried not to collapse onto the floor from the delirious state this unpredictable girl had just put me in. After everything she had put me through, I couldn't be sure if she was being serious or not.

After closing the restaurant, I realized I didn't know the address of Jenny's complex. Running outside, I stopped her just before she was going to ride off on a white bicycle. "Do you like my new bike?" she asked, sounding adorably childlike. I got it at a police auction for twenty dollars."

"It's super," I said. "Jenny, were you serious when you suggested I move into your apartment complex?"

"It's called the Kingwood Manor, and it's at 1146 Third Street," she said, taking off into the night on her bike.

"One one four six Third Street?" I called out.

"Yeah," her voice called out, as she disappeared into the darkness.

I immediately went back inside the restaurant and wrote the address down. I wasn't sure if I was ready to live on my own. I wasn't sure of anything. And now I wasn't even sure who was really making the moves, Jenny, or me.

CHAPTER SIX

I steered my Volkswagen into West Salem around nine o'clock. Only the night before, Jenny had hinted about me moving into her apartment complex. I crossed a couple of side streets until I came to the one that some imaginative genius named Third Street. In seconds I found myself parking in front of the Kingwood Manor. The olive green complex was set up in a single story, open-ended court design. Television antennas decorated the roof, one for each unit. I figured that the place had been built originally in the 1940s. Since then, it had alternated between stages of disrepair and remodeling. I got out of the car and went up to the unit that had the word Manager stenciled above the door in black spray paint. I knocked, but there wasn't any answer. I knocked much louder.

"Coming," yelled a sleepy sounding voice from beyond the door. The door then quickly opened. Standing before me was an elderly woman wearing clothes tailored with a male figure in mind. Her short-cropped gray hair was messed up as if she had recently been in a deep slumber.

Despite this, she looked pleased to see me, even if she didn't have the slightest notion of whom I was. "Hello, I'm Ada Hopkins, and what are you here to do me out of, young man?"

"Well," I started, unsure of myself since I had never rented an apartment before. "I heard something about there being a vacant apartment here."

"I have two vacant apartments, and what about them?"

"I was thinking I might rent one of them."

"I know, young fellow, I was just yanking one of your limbs," Ada said, reaching over to pat me on the head. "Just a second while I fetch my keys, and I'll be happy to show the places off to you." Turning around, she went back into her apartment for a moment. When she returned she was clutching a set of keys in her hand. "I've got two apartments for rent. One's beautiful and clean. The other one's filthy and stinking."

"Excuse me," I asked, not sure I had heard her correctly. "Let me show you number nine," she said, leading me to one of the units. "You see, this ain't any good."

She wasn't being the least bit incorrect in her assessment of the place. The apartment we were in looked like something out of a government film on poverty. Numerous holes decorated the walls and ceiling. Also, there was some kind of petroleum based substance all over the carpets.

"This ain't everything either. Come in here and look at this," the manager said, directing me toward the bedroom.

"Now ain't this the filthiest thing you ever saw?" A large hole had been burned into the bare mattress of an old bed that rested in the center of the room.

"This might just be, ma'am, it just might be. I know that it certainly ranks high on the list," I said. I wondered why I had been brought into that place at all.

"Now that you've seen the slime hole, I'll take you to see the good place." Grabbing me by the arm, she led me out of apartment nine so quickly that I had the feeling that we would be doomed forever if we stayed longer. "What do your folks call you, young fellow?"

"My name is Clark Jackson," I answered, as we went two doors down and stopped in front of number seven.

"What's your line of work, Mr. Jackson?" Ada asked.

She opened the door to this next apartment by sticking her hand through a broken windowpane on the door and unlocking it from the inside.

"I'm a cook at Rod's Hamburgers. By the way, how did that window break?"

"Don't worry none about the window. We'll have it fixed in plenty of time if you decide to move in. So you're the cook at Rod's. That means you know Jenny, who lives over there." Ada pointed straight across the grass to an apartment across from the one that we were entering.

"Yes. She's the one who suggested that I come down and look at these places."

"She's a pretty little girl. Are you two friends? Everyone here just loves her."

"I love her, too." Ada looked at me in a way that told me that she knew what kind of love I was talking about.

"She really is a sweet kid. Well, I better show you this place. As you can see, this one's much better than that other one I just showed you."

It certainly was. Of course, almost anything would have been better than the last apartment we had been in. This one was small, but clean. The living room and the kitchen were in one space. Where the stove began was where the living room was supposed to end. I walked about and found the bedroom through a doorway in the middle of the living room. There I found the bathroom, which instead of having a bathtub had only a shower. I had seen all that I had to see; the only thing important to me of course was that Jenny lived directly across from this place. With that in mind, I turned to the manager and said, "I'll take it."

"Which one? This one rents for $145 every month, while that slime pit I showed you rents for $200."

"I'm going to take this one. That other one's a bit too, uh, big."

"You sure ain't a stupid young fellow, now are you?" Ada remarked, as she led me back to her apartment to fill out the lease.

After finishing the paperwork for the apartment, I headed to downtown Salem. I killed time wandering the sidewalks and browsing in the shops. I was also thinking about the ramifications of what I had done. What would Jenny think about me moving in next door to her? How would she feel? Would she come running into my arms or laugh at me for being a crazy fool?

Around four o'clock, I decided to stop by Rod's. I wasn't scheduled to work, but I hoped to find someone with whom I could discuss my situation with. As I came into the lobby, I saw Jay and Denna sitting together at a table in the corner. I decided to join them.

"Hey, pal, what brings you around here so early?" Jay asked. "Jenny isn't supposed to work for another half hour."

"Does she work tonight?" I asked, trying to appear nonchalant.

"She's supposed to close with Denna here."

"You guys won't believe what I did today," I said.

"I know a guy named Charlie who's in for a bit of disbelief when I get through with him tonight," Denna stated, obviously on another subject.

"I rented the apartment next door to Jenny's."

"That's really slick, Mr. Clark. How did this come about?" Jay asked, with his cat's grin now transformed into that of a leopard's.

"Well, she sort of suggested it to me last night while we were closing, at least I think she did."

Denna looked directly at me, and asked me a question that had little to do with what I wanted to talk about. "Clark, do you think that when a woman goes out with a man for two months she deserves to be told about his wife and five kids?"

"Why, yes, I think that would be a good idea for ...".

"This crumb I've been dating and falling in love with doesn't seem to think it matters. I didn't learn about his other life until his wife paid me a little visit on the phone this morning."

"That's awful," I awkwardly said, not knowing really what to say about Denna's problem. "Is he divorced from this wife?" I asked.

"No!" Denna said, on the verge of releasing moisture from her eyes.

"How do you think Jenny is going to react to my moving in next door to her? I mean, I'm not sure she was being serious when she suggested it," I asked Denna.

"She'll probably react better than Charlie will after I get a hold of him! His wife told me that he lives with her in Hillsboro, and as soon as I get out of here tonight, I'm going there to get him. Only the wife didn't say where he lives, so I'm going to wait for him along the side of the highway. When he comes by on his way home from work, I'll follow that blasted purple Ford pickup of his and surprise him in his driveway."

Jay looked at Denna's red eyes and puffed cheeks and at the anxiety painted on my face. "All I can say is that right this moment I am a very happy man. I don't allow myself to be held hostage by love the way you two unfortunately are."

Denna and I both looked with disdain at Jay, and he wisely got up to head home for the day.

Denna sat quietly, and so did I. Before long, I saw Jenny manning the front counter. She seemed glum about something. I wondered if Jay or someone else told had informed her about what I was up to. I listened hard to make out what the other employees were murmuring about, but it was impossible for me to tell from my distance. I could tell that my Jenny was very depressed about something, and I wanted to go up to her, put my arms around her, and let her know that everything was all right because I loved her. "Jenny looks so sad," I said to Denna. "I don't want her sad, I want her happy. Why can't she realize that?"

"The more I think about it," Denna answered, "the more I feel like forgetting the whole thing and just erasing Charlie from my life altogether. Well, it's about time I dragged myself to work. Tonight's not going to be easy."

We got up and walked together back to the kitchen. I could now hear the assorted whispers of the employees much better, to the point that I would hear "Clark" and "Jenny" repeatedly, each time followed by laughter. I decided to leave before things grew any tenser. I went through the back door just in time to see Jay pulling in with his pickup. "Hi, Jay, what are you doing back here already?"

"I left my sandals in the office, and I wanted to wear them on the date I have tonight. Did you really rent a place next to Jenny, if I may ask?"

"Yes, it's no lie. I've rented the apartment next door to Jenny."

"That's one way to get a girl. Good luck." Jay then ran in to Rod's, and I got in my car and drove home to tell my parents of my plans.

At 9:30 the next morning, I pulled in front of the Kingwood Manor with my Volkswagen filled to its sunroof with personal belongings. Right behind me came my father with his Chevy pickup carrying my bed and other things that would not fit into my vehicle. My parents' reaction to my decision to move out on my own had been favorable. This most likely was because they didn't realize that the whole thing had been inspired by a girl. My mother prepared for me what she called a "care package" consisting of food and household goods. Now my father was helping me with the physical part of my move. I had neglected to ask Ada for a key for the place the day before, so when we tried to get in I had to reach through the broken windowpane. This worried my father.

"You mean they didn't even give you a key to this apartment?" he asked.

"I guess I forgot to ask for one. I'll have to do that after we've finished moving all this junk in."

"They do intend to fix that window, I hope."

I assured Dad that the manager had promised to fix everything and we unloaded all my things and stacked them in the apartment. Dad then took an honest look around the place. "It reminds me of the layout I had in college, before I married your mother," he remarked. "Only that place I had was half as big, and I shared it with a roommate, Buzzy Williams. We had to take turns sleeping and studying, because there wasn't enough room for us to do them at the same time."

"Why didn't you just rent a larger apartment?" I asked.

"I didn't have the money. I wasn't rich then, as I am now." Dad laughed in the way he does when he wants to punctuate a joke, and I laughed with him. He shortly said good-bye, because he had work to do. I watched him get into his pickup and drive off. I began to feel a bit of separation anxiety over the realization that I was no longer quite my parents' child. Sure, I had always felt myself to be very independent, but always with the understanding that my parents would be there as a safety net for me. Now I was on my own, and the grown-up approach to things that I had pretended to have for quite a while would now have to become for real.

CHAPTER SEVEN

I decided that the first thing I should do now that I was on my own was to get a key to my apartment.

"Why, hello, young man," Ada said after I had knocked on her door. "I suppose you'll be wanting a key to your new home."

"Yes. I've gotten my things moved in by reaching through that broken window to open the door. It would be nice to have a key."

"Well, I'll get you one right now. And we'll get that window fixed as soon as Rodger comes around again."

"Rodger?"

"He's the man who owns these apartments. He always likes to take care of any peculiarities that come up himself."

"Oh."

"Here's your key," she said, as she pulled the key off her chain. "You'll be needing a key to the washroom, too, so that you can keep your clothes clean. Have I shown you our washroom?"

"No, I'm afraid you haven't."

"Well, here then, let me show it to you," Ada said, grabbing me by the arm and leading me three doors down. We were about to enter the last door when Jenny suddenly emerged from it, carrying a box full of laundry. She was wearing a bright-red pair of overalls, which accented an unusually deep flushness in her face. There was also a strange, distant gleam in her eyes, particularly when she looked at me.

"Hello, little one. Are you feeling better?" Ada asked Jenny.

"Yes." Jenny responded, in the manner of a schoolgirl answering her teacher.

"How are you doing Jenny?" I asked.

"Fine," Jenny said, her voice dropping off as she looked straight into my eyes. Apparently in an attempt to communicate some message to me. However, I couldn't figure out exactly what this secret message was. She held the eye contact for three or four seconds.

Then she abruptly marched off toward her apartment with her clean load of clothes.

When Jenny was out of hearing range, Ada broke the news bulletin to me. "She said she lost her job at Rod's last night. Is this true?"

"I don't know. I haven't been at Rod's yet today," I said, trying not to show how shocked I was.

"It would be a crying shame if it's true, because she's such a nice girl." Ada then showed me the laundry room, though I wasn't paying any attention. Never in my imagination had I intended for Jenny to lose her job. What sort of creep was I anyway? I'd created a situation that resulted in this girl losing her source of income? I was stupid and selfish, no doubt about it. I must have made her so embarrassed that she was forced to quit. I didn't believe Denna would have fired her. It had to be my fault. As soon as Ada finished giving me instructions on how to operate the apartment complex's thirty-year-old washing machine, I rushed to Jenny's place to make amends. Her door was open, and only her screen door stood between me and the inside of her apartment. I knocked upon the door frame, peering into the apartment. The place was identical to mine, and as I looked, I could not see Jenny. The sound of a radio that sat on the kitchen table was the only trace of life I could make out. I knocked again. This time, Jenny came out of her bedroom, her arms full of laundry.

"What do you want?" she asked, in the manner of a wounded deer. She dropped the laundry onto her dining table and began nervously folding it.

"Jenny, is it true you quit Rod's last night?" I asked, in as polite of voice as I could muster.

"Yes, I did--because of you," she answered, growing angrier in tone.

"Why? I never meant to have you do that."

"Sure you didn't. Why didn't you just leave me alone?

I didn't mind you living here with me. I was trying to be nice to you, because I realize how important it is for people to be on their own. But then you had to go and hurt me, after I tried to help you."

"How did I hurt you?" I asked, while fighting the urge to go climb into a snail's shell.

"You know what you did. You went to Rod's and made a big joke out of me!"

"I didn't mean to hurt you, Jenny."

"Huh! I bet you didn't."

"Could I come inside so we could sit down and discuss this? I'd really like to explain."

"If you don't go away this minute, I'll call the police.

Now leave me alone! Leave me alone, won't you?" Jenny went over and closed the door sharply, but not to the point of slamming it. I slowly dragged myself to my car and started to drive to the one place that could give me the information to figure out exactly what had happened, Rod's.

At Rod's, I found Jay in his office working on the employees' work schedule. "Is it true Jenny quit last night?" I asked.

"She didn't just quit; she walked out in the middle of her shift," Jay said.

"She walked out? Why? Were people saying things about her?"

"Ask Denna about it; she's the one who got stuck high and dry last night. I've got to fill up the gaps on this schedule. We suddenly have a shortage of counter people."

I went out and found Denna making coleslaw in the back. "What happened last night, Denna?" I asked.

"Jenny walked out on me. I gave her a half-hour break, she ordered a fish sandwich, and sat in the lobby. Fifteen minutes later I looked out and saw her leaving. I ran after her, yelling that she wasn't going to walk out on me. But she kept walking straight ahead, as if she didn't even hear me."

"Were the other girls making fun of her or something?"

"They were talking about your renting that apartment. The girls weren't being cruel about it, you know how nice our girls are, Clark."

"Jenny looked pretty upset about something that was going on last night." "I think that girl finally realized you were serious about her, and she got scared. That's what I think, at least."

"It makes sense, I guess, that she'd be scared. After all, the way I've been chasing after her...".

"It's not every day someone will just walk away from their job like that. There could be something else the matter with that girl." Denna stopped, as if she were going into an area that she didn't want to discuss with me.

"What else might be the matter with Jenny, Denna?"

"Oh, nothing. She's a little scared, that's all," Denna said.

She brought a flickering smile to her face.

So everything might just be my fault, I thought. If I had been good enough to leave the girl alone when she had asked me to, she wouldn't have become scared enough to lose her job. I had been too aggressive. Because of my own inflated skull, I had now lost Jenny forever. I quietly thanked Denna for filling me in on the situation, and walked shamefully out to my car. It was hard for me not to cry as I drove to the apartments.

As I walked along the short patch of sidewalk that existed between my car and my apartment, I was careful not to look towards Jenny's place. I knew that I would surely melt into nothing if I were to see her again this day--my heart could only stand so much. I tried my key to see if it worked, which it did. For the first time, I took a real look around the place I was to be calling my homestead. I checked the kitchen cupboards, deciding what variety of food should be kept where. Next came the hanging of my shower curtain, followed by the examination of my sole clothes closet. I reached out and grabbed the clothes hanger rod to see how strong it was. It came off in my hand. "Grand," I thought, as I replaced the rod and gingerly placed my shirts on it.

I fiddled around unpacking for several hours before putting on my work clothes and leaving for Rod's. Outside, as I started toward my car, I dared to look over my shoulder at Jenny's place. She could be seen in her window, sitting in a rocking chair, staring forlornly back at me. She looked like the most depressed person in the entire history of humanity. In truth I was, because it was my fault Jenny was unhappy.

The first week I spent as an independent adult started mundanely. My life alternated between being a hired hand at Rod's and being a captive within the walls of my apartment. I slowly unpacked, getting my belongings set up exactly the way I felt they should be. When I wasn't organizing my things, I was watching television--anything to keep from thinking of Jenny.

On the fourth day after the move, as I sat in an old brown easy chair lent to me by Ada, I gazed through a slight crack I had made in my drape. Having grown up on a farm, it was hard getting used to strangers peering in at me. My eyes were focused, of course, upon Jenny's place. Since I had moved in, I hadn't seen Jenny, with the exception of that one night of sadness, and I had come to believe she had moved away. Suddenly, though, as I watched her door, I saw it open, and out came Jenny. What's more, she was walking straight toward my place! She stood outside my door for a moment, looking as if she were debating whether to knock. Before she could come to any decision, she glanced my direction and detected my knowledge of her presence. I immediately got out of the easy chair and walked away from the window. It was too late, though, because the sound of Jenny's door slamming rang out across the court and into my ears. My hopes, which so suddenly had been resurrected, were now again crucified. Feeling the need to at least temporarily escape my small prison, I decided to go to a local convenience store and get a Mars bar.

When I returned a few minutes later, I finally understood what Jenny had been up to before. That was because there was an envelope taped to my door just below the broken window-pane. Jenny must have seen me leave and returned to accomplish the mission she had been trying to complete earlier, before I had scared her off. Having a feeling Jenny was watching, I decided to take the envelope inside before reading the note.

Dear Clark,
I am very sorry about what happened between us earlier this week. You didn't deserve to be treated the way I treated you. I wouldn't blame you if you didn't like me anymore, but since we are now neighbors, we might as well be friends. Anytime you feel like coming over, you are welcome to visit with me.
Jenny

"Thank stars for Mars bars!" I thought, as if Jenny would never have gotten her message to me if I hadn't developed a craving for candy. Of course, I wanted to scramble over to Jenny's for a visit the moment I was finished reading the note. But I had allowed my tendency to rush things with Jenny in the past to almost destroy any chance of having a relationship with her. This time I vowed to be more patient and wait until the next morning before taking up Jenny on her offer.

I woke at 8:30 the next morning, showered, shaved carefully, and got dressed for Rod's, where I had to be at 11:30. I figured that my work commitment would provide good way to keep myself from spending too much time with Jenny. Not that I didn't want to spend as much time as possible with her, it was simply part of my new plan to keep things short and sweet with Jenny and not rush her into a relationship with me. At 9:30, I approached Jenny's apartment, steadied myself, and knocked gently upon her door. It opened immediately, and my dream girl brightly smiled when she saw that it was me. "Hi, Jenny," I said, starting a sentence I had been practicing all morning. "I got your note last night, but I'm afraid I can't accept your apology...".

"Why not?" Jenny asked with a trembling voice.

"Unless you accept mine first."

Jenny, laughing affectionately in acceptance of my apology, turned and looked into her apartment. "Everything is nice and neat in here, so if you want, you can come in unless you would rather stay out there." Briefly glancing back at me, she walked into her place, and I quickly followed. "Do you want iced tea or Kool Aid?" she asked, after having me sit at her kitchen table.

"Iced tea," I answered, "I have to get my daily supply of caffeine."

"I like iced tea, too," Jenny said, as she poured us a couple of large glasses of it. "I only keep the Kool Aid in the refrigerator for guests who don't want tea."

We talked lightly and warmly for the next hour and a half, never really saying very much at all. When I excused myself to go to work, though, there was a mutual sense of connection between us. No longer was I alone in my feelings. Now Jenny seemed to be on the same wavelength and was as sensitive to my presence as I had always been to hers. Saying goodbye was difficult, but I stuck to my resolution of keeping things brief and sweet. Somehow I managed to cut myself loose from the glowing attractions of Jenny long enough to make it to my car.

I quickly was driving along the same stretch of street that I had driven four days earlier, when my situation with Jenny had seemed hopeless. The weather this day was equal to the prior one. The sun was overhead, and the waters of the Willamette shone directly across from me. It was almost as good as a movie.

Jenny's Diary

It surely is funny how things turn out sometimes. I was so mad at Mom for telling me I had to find my own place now. She knew if I did, I wouldn't just be able to quit that burger place as I wanted to. Then Clark actually listened to my suggestion, and moved in here next to me! It was perfect. He's so unlike the guys I've known before. He really is smart. But he really seems to love me. I think I can love him too. So I up and quit Rods anyway. Clark will take care of me.

CHAPTER EIGHT

Pausing first to straighten our fancy Tuxedos, my best man and I walk into the sanctuary of a large house of worship, followed by several groomsmen. Positioning ourselves on the right side of a large altar, we watch as a string quartet begins strumming some music by Handel. Then a procession of beautiful bridesmaids walk down the center aisle. And then comes Jenny, dressed from head to toenail in fine silk. Once Jenny reaches the front, a clergyman asks, "Who gives this woman?"

"I do," states the man who escorted Jenny up the aisle.

The man then releases Jenny and sits. Jenny stares into my eyes, and I into hers, and we become one.

This is what I had in mind when asking Jenny to marry me. However, this had about as much to do with reality as bubble gum has to do with T-bone steak.

The days that followed our Saturday morning discussion are blurred in my memory in a haze of romantic frenzy. We spent every minute together we could. At first we found convenient excuses. Once, I needed her help with the washing machine. Another time she needed my sauce pan. Soon, we stopped needing excuses, and just got together because we felt like it. There seemed no need to keep things slow after all. Jenny was as interested in me as I was in her.

"I thought you'd never get here," Jenny said one night, though I was five minutes early. "Dinner's ready." Her table was set, and our meal was waiting. Sitting at the table, we were about to eat when I noticed she was looking at me with a curious expression. "Aren't you going to say grace?"

"In my family we only said grace at Thanksgiving," I replied, digging into the food.

"Oh," Jenny said, helping herself to her food as well.

It wasn't until Jenny started clearing the table after dinner that I noticed a paper object on the table. A cardboard automobile model cut out off the back of a cereal box. It was a VW Bug, and the right fender had been tom to resemble mine. And on the side were the words "I love you, Clark," in Jenny's handwriting. I felt like reaching over and pulling Jenny into my arms right then, but something held me back. It might be better, I decided, to wait until Jenny told me directly. I pretended not to have noticed the cardboard model.

"Only Ada would furnish an apartment with a couch as big as this," I said, after we had moved to the seven-foot-long brown couch in Jenny's living room.

"Oh, this couch is mine," Jenny said. "It's the same one you caught my mom sleeping on. When they moved, they couldn't get it through the door, so they brought it over here."

Though it was still early, the sound of someone snoring leaked through the wall behind our heads.

"That's the old lady who lives next door," Jenny said, smiling. "She has really bad emphysema."

"Is she one of the ladies who work in the canneries?"

"Yeah. Most of the ladies who live here work in the canneries."

"What do they do when the canneries close down for the season?"

"They collect unemployment."

"That sounds pretty bleak."

"What do you mean?"

"I've never seen anyone at Rod's lose a finger the way people sometimes do at a cannery."

"The pay, along with the unemployment, works out to be more than I make at Rod's."

"The last thing I'd ever want to see you do is become one of these cannery ladies."

"Why not?" Jenny asked, her face full of astonishment.

"They seem so lonely. I don't want that to happen to you. I want you to be loved, and have someone who takes care of you."

"I," Jenny said, tears building in her eyes, "I don't want to be like that either." I boldly tried to pull her face up so I could look into her eyes, but Jenny yanked her whole body away from me. "Why don't you just go away and leave me alone," she screamed. Instantly, she ran to the table, wadded up the cardboard model, and tossed it at me. I watched the wrecked model hit the carpet in front of me, and felt like screaming too.

"Okay, that's it, Jenny," I said, rising from the couch. "I'm tired of you lying to me. Either you like me or you don't. Both can't be true. What do you want me to believe, what you said just now, or what you wrote on that model car you just destroyed?" A small, embarrassed smile came to Jenny's lips. "I want to think you like me, but I guess I'll never know because you don't have the guts to tell me. I just hope someday you have enough courage to let someone have an idea how you really feel about them." At this point I lost the ability to speak, so I started for the door.

As I reached for the door, though, Jenny said softly but firmly "No, don't go." I froze, and Jenny rushed to me. "I do want to be your girl," she said, looking embarrassed. "And..., I love you." And without saying more, we awkwardly kissed for the first time.

I had kissed girls before, but no kiss had ever felt like this one. Jenny's shy lips trembled as they pressed against mine. As we wrapped our arms gently around each other, it was like we had become a giant mass of romantic unity. When we finally pulled our lips apart for breathing purposes, Jenny couldn't have found room for a bigger smile on her tiny face. "You sure know to kiss a girl," she said.

"I like your lips too." I gazed deep into her sweet blue eyes, not believing she was finally my girl. And my emotions overran me. I'd wanted her to be my girl so much, and for what seemed so long. And she had been so hot and cold in her attitudes toward me that I was desperate to keep her now that I had her. "Jenny," I said somberly. "You don't have to give me an answer right away, but will you marry me?" Jenny's face went blank, and I knew I'd spoken too fast. "You feel like some ice cream?" I asked quickly. "I'm in the mood for chocolate chip."

"Yes," Jenny said.

"You feel like chocolate chip, too?"

"Yes, Clark, I will marry you, and be your wife."

I stood stunned. I had gotten what I wanted, but instead of feeling elated, I was curiously flustered. "Well," I finally said. "In the movies, at a moment like this, they usually kiss." So we did.

CHAPTER NINE

"Yes, I'd like to speak with Darrel Hankman, please," I said to the guy who answered the phone in Darrel's college dorm.

"Hello," Darrel finally said, after a two minute wait.

"Darrel?" I asked, to make sure it was him.

"Clark! How are you?"

"Fine. Look, I'm here on campus. I don't know where your dorm is."

"Where are you?"

"In the student center."

"Where are you in Riley?"

"Riley?"

"That's the name of the building you're in. The one that in your ignorance you called the student center."

"Oh. Right now I'm in the snack bar."

"You mean the Burger Basket. Wait there, and I'll be right over."

The receiver clicked. I found a booth, sat, and waited as directed. Darrel was finished with the convenience store, and was in his first days of attending college. I had driven out to ask him to be my best man.

Darrel came bursting into the Burger Basket, his light-brown hair in a disheveled wet mess, and his shirt unbuttoned in front. He glanced around the Burger Basket until he saw me. "You've gotta excuse me," he said as he plopped down across the table from me. "I was just getting out of the shower when you called." It was two in the afternoon, but Darrel was well known for keeping an unusual schedule when it came to stuff such as showers. "Well, what brings you here?" Darrel asked, as he started running a comb though his hair.

"I'm getting married," I announced.

Darrel was so surprised he failed to stop his comb when it reached a particularly tangled knot of hair. Though he had nearly removed an important part of his hairline, he didn't utter a sound. "Who?" He asked, massaging his scalp.

"This girl I met at Rod's. Her name is Jenny Whittington."

"When?"

"A week and a half from now, on the twenty-ninth."

"W-why?"

"Because, we want to."

"Parents?"

"Hers are happy. Mine are really ticked off."

"Expecting?"

"No chance, of that until we're married. And will you quit with the one word questions? You sound like you're either taking a journalism class or training to be a cop with the Los Angeles Police Department."

"Are you sure about this, Clark?"

"What do you mean?"

"What happened to the guy who once said he wouldn't marry until he was fifty?"

"I don't know. I guess I lied."

"And what do you want from me?"

"Will you be my best man?"

"Of course, I'll be. So your family's not very happy about this?"

"My mom was a little upset. She ran to her bedroom and slammed the door."

"Dad?"

"He told Jenny she wasn't going to get her hands on any of his money. Other than that, he wished us luck. Then my mom came out and did the same, though it was obvious she still wasn't very happy."

"I'm amazed your parents caved in. I think this whole thing sounds stupid. But I'll be there for you. Now, where's the wedding taking place?"

"At some Baptist Church. I'll give you the address as soon as I learn what it is."

"Is this girl religious?" Darrel asked, acting as if he were saying a dirty word.

"I don't think so. She told me that she joined this church just so she would have a place to get married."

"A girl who comes equipped with her own church. That's something."

"I love her, Darrel."

"I'm sorry. It's just that this whole deal sprang up so quickly. You must do these things because you were hyper-active as a child. I'd like to meet this girl sometime before the wedding, but there isn't much time."

"Sure, we can do that this week."

"I'm really looking forward to meeting Joanie."

"It's Jenny." We decided there wasn't time for a bachelor's party. Then Darrel noticed he was late for a class, and I had to get back to Salem for the night shift at Rod's.

CHAPTER TEN

"That's it," I screamed. "We'll just have to call the wedding off!"

"I'm sorry," Jenny wailed through her tears. "I've spent a lot of time making this place into a home, and I don't see why I have to be the one who moves."

"The reason is simple. I like my apartment better, and I think we should live there."

With two days to go before the wedding, Jenny and I had reached a major impasse. We weren't going to need two apartments. One of us was going to have to move.

"You've hardly lived in your apartment," Jenny sobbed.

"It's cold there. Cold and empty. I always get the strange feeling someone was murdered there once. My apartment feels different. It feels warm and full of the Lord."

"Don't you go bringing God into this," I said, almost snarling. "For the last couple of weeks you and your mother have been really pushing for us to have the song "We've Only Just Begun" played at the ceremony as well."

"Well, can you think of a better song?"

I tried to think, but couldn't. "No," I finally said. "It's just the idea. I've always liked being different from everyone else, that's all."

"Why do you want to be different? Besides, it's too late to change the song now. Getting back to where we'll be living, I'd like to ask you something."

"Well, ask."

"Where have we spent most of our time the last two weeks?"

"At your place."

"Where are we right now?"

"Your place."

"So where do you think we should live?"

"My place." Without saying more, I charged out of her apartment.

Instead of returning to my own place, I walked. That's what I remember most. I walked through the black night air, block after block. I have no idea why I was so angry. I just wanted my own way, like a spoiled child, I guess. After walking fifteen blocks, I calmed down. And realized I was being a fool. Here I had my dream girl, and I was walking out on her. In my pocket was five dollars. Not much to buy a peace offering with. At this time of night, not much was open, either. I turned a corner, and there, right in front of me, glowed a giant red Safeway grocery store sign. Five dollars should buy something here, I hoped.

Returning to the scene of the crime, I hesitated outside Jenny's door, and decided for the moment to hide the bag I'd hauled from the store. I had just tucked the sack behind a bush when Jenny pulled open her door. But she didn't say anything. She just stared at me with eyes so intense I thought they would eventually burn me. I could tell she'd been wailing.

"Can I come in?"

"It was your choice to leave." She stepped back from the door, and I tip-toed inside.

"I'm sorry I walked out," I said softly.

"I'm used to it," she said. "Everybody always leaves me."

"I won't," I said, feeling horrible. She looked so scared. I tried to pull her into my arms, but she moved out of reach. I decided if there was a time she needed a surprise, this was it.

"Where are you going?" Jenny asked as I headed out the door.

Without answering, I leaned outside and picked up the sack. "I got you something," I said, holding the bag out to her.

"You did?" From the look on her face, I could see it didn't matter that her present was wrapped in an ugly grocery sack. She grabbed it from me.

"Careful," I said. Glancing in the bag, she cautiously pulled the contents out. "They're African Violets," I said, as Jenny looked at the potted plant with the colorful blossoms.

"A boy's never given me flowers before," she said.

"That's hard to believe," I said.

"They're bright and pretty," Jenny said. And so was her face. "What did you say they're called?"

"African Violets. Haven't you heard of them before?"

"No."

"I wanted to get you a rose or something, but Safeway was out."

"But I like these better than some rose that'll just dry up." Staring down at the pot, she smiled bigger. "I'll be sure to water these, and keep them alive forever. The same way I'll always love you."

The last part was said under her breath, as if she dreaded letting me hear it. I wanted to tug on my ears to make sure they were working. She lovingly set the violets on her dinette table, and grabbed me as if I was a big teddy bear. Our lips joined, and I knew I adored her more than anything I had ever known. "I love you," I said.

"I love you too, Clark. So are you moving in here?"

"No. We're moving into my place."

Jenny burst into a new set of tears. "Could you tell me why?"

"Because your shower has a crummy showerhead," I said, feeling stupid about the whole deal. "I mean, my place has a better nozzle on the showerhead. Your shower is about the same as standing beneath a garden hose."

"Your place hardly ever has hot water. That's why you're always using my shower."

"Yes, but when I do have hot water, my shower is better."

Jenny's tears changed into laughter as I stood there sounding like a fool. "Clark, why don't we just move away from here, and into a better complex?"

I just nodded my head, knowing this was the only way we could end the argument. I hated the apartments we were living in anyway.

My last night as a free man was spent rehearsing to become the opposite. The church was actually a large tent like structure that was intended to be temporary. However, Jenny said that every time a plan for a new building was submitted to the congregation, the people would reject it. They always decided the temporary structure was better. Eventually, the temporary building had become permanent.

"Well, here's the young couple," the Rev. Carl Allen said as we walked into the church. Pastor Allen had paid us a visit a few days before, and was horrified at the only reason we gave for getting married. And this was because we wanted to. "Are you two ready for your big moment?" he asked, putting one of his arms around each of us.

"Hopefully," I answered.

Upon entering the worship hall, I noticed a sizable gathering of people, none of whom I knew. It turned out they were all from Jenny's family. I had told my family not to bother showing up for the rehearsal. Even Darrel wasn't there yet. The only people in this mob that I recognized were Jenny's mom and stepfather. I felt like we should go say hi to them. Before we could, though, a middle-aged man came up to us. He held out his arms to Jenny, after a moment of hesitation she flew into them. "Hi, Daddy," she said when the hug was over.

"Hello, Jennifer. How have you been doing?" the man asked.

"Fine. Have you met Rev. Allen?" asked Jenny.

"Yes, we have," answered her father, while glaring at the pastor.

"It seems your father is superior to me in knowing the Bible," said Rev. Allen.

"I just think that a man in your line of work should know the Scripture," responded Jenny's dad.

The two men stood staring at each other with synthetic smiles for a few seconds. Jenny told me later that her father distrusted any connection with organized religion. As if she were used to it, Jenny quickly changed the subject. "Dad, this is Clark Jackson, the man I am marrying tomorrow."

"Well, it's good to finally stare into the whites of your eyes," he said to me.

"It's good to meet you too, sir," I said, offering my hand and struggling to keep smiling as he glared at me.

"I've always wondered what sort of fool would marry Jenny," he said. It was hard to tell if he was joking.

Before the conversation became more involved, Rev. Allen decided it was time we started what we came there for, namely rehearse for the wedding. The practice was easy enough for me, since all that I had to do was take ten steps after entering the hall from a side door.

We went through our basic movements a couple of times. We were about to try them for a third when Darrel came busting into the Worship Hall, shouting. "Clark, do you have to get married in a place like this?" One of Darrel's problems was that he would often speak first and realize where he was second. Of course, this time it did not take him long to realize that of all the times to do such a thing, he had picked the most embarrassing. To my relief, no one made any inquiries into what Darrel had said, and the matter was forgotten.

The rehearsal ended shortly after that because we didn't practice the vows. We didn't even know what they were. All we had to do at the wedding was repeat them after Rev. Allen said them. He told us he felt they would be special to us if we only heard them for the first time as we became one.

Jenny's family gathered around us in front of the altar. I was introduced to her stepmother, her five sisters, and her two brothers. I introduced Jenny to Darrel, and as they talked, Mr. Whittington asked me over to a corner to discuss doing him a favor.

"Well, you see," he said, once we were away from the others, "my wife and I don't know Salem very well. And I was wondering if you could direct us to a motel."

"There is a nice one downtown called...".

"We don't want anything fancy. We're simple people who like to live inexpensively."

"Let me see, there's a whole bunch of motels out on Commercial Street.

You could probably find one you like out there."

"Commercial Street, now how do I get there from here?"

"When you pull out of the parking lot here, you head down Market Street. It'll lead you straight to Commercial.

"I think I'll remember those directions tonight, son. However, you see, I sort of have this trick memory, and by tomorrow, I may have forgotten how to get back here. I wonder, do you suppose you could wait for me in your car at the turnoff I'll need to make so I won't miss it?"

I did think that it was strange that a man who could correct a minister on the Bible would have trouble remembering simple directions. I guessed, though, that he wouldn't have asked me for help if he didn't need it. "Sure, I'll be glad to wait for you."

"You're a regular lifesaver. That's what you are, son, a real lifesaver. What kind of car do you drive?"

"A gold Volkswagen Beetle. You can't miss it, the right fender was smashed up by a deer."

"You want to marry my little girl and you can't even drive a German golf cart?" Mr. Whittington caught himself, and inhaled deeply. "Okay, I'll be driving by at twelve o'clock." We shook hands and went back to the altar area, where Jenny and Darrel were still talking. "Looks like the best man is trying to steal the bride," Mr. Whittington joked. "Jennifer, how about going out with me to my car. I've brought you something."

"You did, Daddy?" Jenny said, in the way some children sound when their daddies give them presents.

When Jenny and her father left the hall, Darrel grabbed me by the shoulder. He led me back to the same corner I had managed to escape from only moments before. "What's so important, Darrel?" I asked when he finally let go of me.

"It's this girl you're seeing."

"Jenny?"

"You really don't intend to marry her, do you?"

"Well, since there is a wedding scheduled for us tomorrow, I would say that we are going to get married."

"Like I said before, I don't see why you don't want to just live with the girl for a while."

There were times when I wondered why Darrel and I called each other friends, and this was one of those moments. "All I know," I said, after pausing to think for a second, "is that I want to marry Jenny. That's all there is to it."

"You haven't even known her for that long. I don't know, it just seems that there's something wrong with her."

"Like what?"

"Like the way she moves her eyes. Sometimes she doesn't move them because she's reacting to something. Sometimes they jerk around in their sockets for no reason at all."

"We all do a bit of that, Darrel, especially when we're nervous about something. We can be pretty sure Jenny has a good reason for being nervous, she's becoming my wife tomorrow."

"Are you sure I can't talk you out of it?" Darrel asked with a surrendering smile.

"I don't think anybody can."

"Well, I had to give it a try anyway," Darrel said. He shrugged in a way that made me realize that he had simply been testing me the entire time.

When it was time for the evening to end, Jenny went to spend the night' at her mother's. I went home alone to

spend many hours in a concentrated
study of the paint on the ceiling above
my bed.

Jenny's Diary

Finally, I'm getting hitched. Never thought it was ever going to happen. But now it is. I'm so scared. I remember when I first knew I wanted to get married. I was playing with my dolls. I should say, my sister's dolls. My Daddy wouldn't buy me a doll of my own. He said he's already bought his family enough dolls, and that I had to make do with ones on hand. It wasn't fair that he wouldn't even buy me one doll. But then I realized that someday I would get married and have babies, and that my babies would be my very own! I've wanted to be married for so long. But what if it fails? What if Clark gets to know me and hates me? Well, I hope to God that he will have least given me a baby by that time.

CHAPTER ELEVEN

Clark Jackson's Journal

A wedding day. I'd long dreamed of the day I would have the girl of my dreams become my wife. I'd always believed it would be one of the best days of my life....

I was rudely awakened by my clock radio at nine o'clock. After having my traditional cold cereal and instant coffee I showered, shaved, and spent two frantic hours combing my hair. I knew that I should have found the time to go to a barber, but somehow there simply hadn't been enough time to do so lately. When my hair finally was as neat as I could manage to get it without shaving it off, I buttoned up a new white shirt my father had given me. Then I put on my best and only suit. It was the same blue suit I had worn to my high school graduation. Since this wedding had turned out to be a very casual affair, I figured this suit would do the trick again. When I finally finished dressing, I got an old grocery bag and packed a few essentials in it. Jenny, and I planned to go off on an adventure somewhere after the wedding. This done, I made my way out to my car. I took the bag and hid it on the floor of the backseat. Then I threw a coat over it, just so nobody at the wedding would know exactly what we had planned. Now it was twelve fifteen, and I felt I was right on schedule, since the wedding was supposed to start at one thirty.

I drove to a gas station two blocks away and had the VW's tank filled. Then I drove to the spot where I had agreed to meet Mr. Whittington and waited for him. After waiting a half hour, I began to get the feeling that I had missed him. He knew what time the wedding was supposed to be, and he had said that he would be coming down Commercial on his way to the church at twelve. Then I came to the realization that I was the one who was late. I guessed that I had been thinking that we were supposed to meet at one instead of twelve. "Oh, this is just great," I thought. "My future father-in-law is now most likely lost somewhere in Salem all because I got my times mixed up!" Knowing how complex the street system was in Salem, I knew that it was very possible that Mr. Whittington could find himself in the Pacific Ocean before he realized that he had missed me. Since it would have been utterly hopeless for me to try searching for him in the short time that remained I elected to drive to the church. Even I knew that it is harder to do without a groom at a wedding than it is a father of the bride.

I pulled into the church a few minutes later, parking so awkwardly my Bug filled two parking spaces. No sooner had I parked when Darrel came rushing out of the church to meet me.

"Where?" Darrel asked tensely.

"I've been waiting for Mr. Whittington at the intersection of Commercial and Market," I replied. I climbed out of my car. "I'm afraid we missed each other, and Jenny's father is probably lost somewhere."

"Nope."

"Mr. Whittington's not lost? You mean he's here?"

"Sure."

"I don't believe it."

"He's been here a couple of hours, getting things ready. He's been telling us repeatedly how great it is for him to be back in the town he grew up in."

"He grew up here? But, Darrel, last night he asked me for directions to a motel. Then he asked me to help him and his wife find their way back here today."

"Weird," Darrel said. "He's also jawing about how he and his wife spent the night at the home of one of his old friends."

"I don't understand."

"It doesn't matter. Instead of discussing the effects of anxiety upon your paranoid imagination, let's get inside. You're scheduled to do something stupid in fifteen minutes."

We scrambled into the church, pausing briefly to comb our hair at a small mirror just inside the front door. We walked into the sanctuary, which to my surprise was filled with people. "Hi," said one lady sitting in the front pew, whom I had never seen before.

"Hi," Darrel and I both said, as we hurried into the Pastor's office. Darrel went into the office, but before I did my father motioned for me to come back to where he was sitting near the back. I was surprised by how happy he seemed.

"Dad, why are you sitting way in the back?"

"All the closer seats were taken," he said, smiling. "This girl you're marrying must have a large family."

"Yeah," I said. "Where's Mom?"

"She's back trying to help set up for the reception."

"Reception?"

"What you do after the ceremony."

"Oh."

"It's good to have you here, Dad."

"I wouldn't miss this for anything, son." He then slapped some cash into my hand. "That's to pay the minister with," Dad said. Then he handed me an even larger lump. "This is for Jenny and you."

"Thanks, Dad," I said.

"Well, you'd better be getting to where you need to be." I walked slowly away and back toward the Pastor's office.

"Hi," again said the lady I didn't know.

"Hi," I answered.

"Oh, Clark, you look so handsome," Jenny's mom said as soon 'as I walked into the office. She went right to work pinning a white carnation on my lapel."

"Thanks. By the way, who is the friendly lady in front pew?"

Jenny's mom peeked out the door. "I don't know," she said. "I thought all those people were from your side of the family."

"Oh."

"I'm so glad you showed up, Clark. I really didn't expect you to." Jenny's mom walked out before I could ask her why she felt that way.

Rev. Allen rose from behind his desk. "Are you ready, Chris?"

"It's Clark."

"Oh, sorry about that," he said, scratching out the name he had written on his notes and replacing it with the proper one.

Then I reached out and shook his hand, slipping him the money like I'd seen people do in movies. "I'm ready if you're ready, Minister."

"Well, you didn't have to pay me my fee now," Rev. Allen said, looking extremely embarrassed. "Why, this looks like a great deal of money," he said.

"I'm sorry, sir, I gave you the wrong money," I said, plucking the money right of his palm and replacing it with the smaller amount.

At one thirty the wedding began. A solo pianist played We've Only Just Begun. I was amazed at how moving the song seemed in this setting, and I no longer regretted having it played. Karen Carpenter, the lady famous for singing it, was pretty nice looking, too. Then I froze, not believing myself. Here it was my wedding, and I was thinking about another woman. After the song was finished, Rev. Allen came out and stood in front of his podium, glancing at his watch and looking as if he had some better place to be. Then, to my shock, an entire choir marched in and started singing some old hymn I'd never heard before.

"I didn't know we were going to have a choir," I whispered to Darrel.

"If you had gotten here on time, you would have known why," Darrel hissed back.

"Well, why are they singing?"

"They have to be here to sing at the Pastor's daughter's wedding, which is two hours after yours."

"Is that why there are so many people here?"

"Yes," Darrel whispered, looking at me like I was a total fool.

"My father sure looks happy."

"Yes, he looks happier about this bit of insanity you're committing than you do. And you'd better shut up. It's rude to talk while a choir is singing." Darrel's voice, though, was almost louder than that of the entire choir combined.

The choir finished. Then, sounding like thunder crashing down from an angry God, the pianist fell into a rousing rendition of the wedding march. Darrel and I both grew rigid, as if we were about to march to the electric chair.

A second later, Denna nervously came down the aisle in a cream colored dress. The dress looked perfect, and Denna, being Denna, was having a difficult time keeping her tears inside. After Denna made it down the aisle, Jenny emerged on her father's arm. Her hair was painstakingly prepared, showing off her blond curls. She was wearing full makeup, and I liked it, having not once before seen a single cosmetic on her face. Her white dress, though it was better suited for an office than for a wedding, looked wondrous anyway. It was the first time I'd seen her in a dress.

Jenny trembled with nervousness as she came down the aisle. She shook from her curls to her open toed shoes.

"Who gives this woman?" Pastor Allen asked. "I do," Jenny's father said.

"I give her away too!" Jenny's mother yelled, from her seat of honor in the fifth row of pews. Leaving Jenny at my side, Mr. Whittington sat as far away as he could from his former wife.

Darrel gave me a glance that suggested there was still time for us to make a dash for the doors, but I ignored it.

"Marriage isn't for the faint of heart," Pastor Allen said, addressing the congregation. "That is why I'm pleased Clark and Jennifer have spent a great deal of time considering the responsibilities which they are taking on today." Darrel snickered so loudly that Pastor Allen stopped and stared at him. He slapped his face with his hand to sober himself up, and Pastor Allen continued with the vows. "Clark, will you take Jennifer to be your wife?"

"I will," I said, trying to sound brave.

"Then repeat the following after me. Jennifer."

"Jennifer."

"I promise to be your friend in everything."

"I promise to be your friend in everything," I repeated.

I hated our vows, but what was I to do?

"Your friends will be my friends."

"Your friends will be my friends."

"And hand-in-hand we will walk through the hills and valleys of our relationship."

"And hand-in-hand we will...". As I said the last line of our vows, I wished we'd taken time to find better ones. But there wasn't anything we could do about it now. And as Jenny repeated the vows to me, I decided it didn't matter. My dream girl was now mine for real, and forever.

"I now pronounce you husband and wife," Pastor Allen said. I kissed Jenny, and we marched arm in arm down the aisle. We raced to the fellowship hall, where a small reception was to be held. -

"You did it, old man," a smiling Darrel said, shaking my hand.

"It's too bad Jay couldn't have been here to see this," a tearful Denna said.

"Well" he really wanted to finish that wood cabinet he's been working on at home, I said.

"You have quite a handsome husband, Mrs. Jackson," an elderly lady said to Jenny.

"Ellie, you beat me again," said another elderly lady.

"You see," she explained, "we like to compete with each other to see who's going to call a bride by her new name first. Ellie beat me again."

We had less than a half hour to cut our cake, shake a few hands, and make certain the forms were filled out right. Then Jenny and I climbed into the one eyed VW, and drove off to begin the rest of our lives.

CHAPTER TWELVE

After a one night honeymoon at the Super 12 Motel, where they like to make a big deal about including clean towels in the room price, Jenny and I settled down in our new home life. Which included a fancy new apartment. The place was three times the cost of the ones we'd been renting from Ada, but it also three times as big, and had just been built. We gave the manager half the cash we had in the world, and he gave us the keys. Then manager went with us to show us how to turn on the heat. However, when he tried to turn on the main heater, the manager nearly electrocuted himself. "You okay?" I asked.

"Yes. Barely. But I'm afraid there won't be any heat in this unit until I can get a guy to look at this."

"Can we move in, anyway?" Jenny asked.

"Sure. You've paid for the place. But it's barely above freezing outside, Miss."

"That's Mrs., and we'll manage," Jenny said.

The most common wedding gift we had received was blankets, and we used every one our first weekend in that frozen apartment. But Jenny was right. It was still better the Kingwood Manor apartments. And as we broke in our wedding present dishes, it was as if we, were a prince and princess, reigning over a kingdom limited only by the size of our dreams.

November 10, 1980

Our dream home was perfect. We didn't have a dining room, and our bed was a chunk of foam rubber. But we didn't need furniture. We had love. But what we didn't have, and what I was growing more and more worried about, was our lack of money. Jay had given me a raise of forty cents an hour, but I wasn't getting nearly enough hours to pay all our bills. After paying the rent, electricity, and phone bills, we had little money for even food.

Jenny didn't seem to care, though. She would greet me with a kiss when I came home from a shift, and make everything seem okay.

On days that I didn't have to work until the evening, we would head downtown and look in the furniture stores and the mall, always browsing, never buying. I would watch Jenny's face glow as she saw things she wanted, and I felt so bad that I couldn't afford to buy them for her. Not working at Rod's.

November 15, 1980

Coming home from another shift, I found Jenny on the couch. Her tears were flying all over the room. "My Mom is moving to Arizona," she cried.

"That's too bad. Did she say why?"

"She doesn't need a reason. Every time we get settled somewhere, she decides to move again. I've never been able to stay in one place very long."

"But Jenny, you're with me now. You don't have to move."

"That's what's so awful. She just married me off so she could move away without me."

"I'm sorry," I said, thinking how strange it was that they would move away with so little warning. Two weeks later they were gone, leaving us with twenty bucks and a dinette set they didn't wish to take with them. Then they drove off, leaving Jenny all to me.

December 22, 1980

Jay was having a Christmas party. Everyone from the Rod's world was there. Even Rod Casum, the Rod of Rod's, stopped by for five minutes. I knew it was five minutes because he had set his fancy wristwatch alarm for exactly that amount of time. He ran back to his limo the second the alarm went off. "Rod hates to spend more time than necessary at parties," Jay explained.

"But it seems really silly for him to spend all that time putting on tails, just to spend five minutes with us," I said, shaking my head.

"Yes, but look at all the money he has, and look at how little you have," Jay said. Jenny nodded her head, and

117

suddenly I was furious at Jay. But he was my boss, and I had to keep my mouth shut.

"Clark," said Shannon a little later in the evening. "When you first showed up to be trained at my restaurant, I didn't give you a chance in a million of making it. But you proved me wrong."

"Thanks," I said softly.

"You know, when you and Jenny were being trained together at my store, I secretly thought you two would wind up getting married."

"You did?"

"I mean, it's just that you two look so much alike. You two are going to have the cutest babies."

"Yeah," Jenny said, looking excited.

"I guess," I said. I couldn't afford to support us as it was.

A baby was the furthest thing from my mind. But from the look on Jenny's face, I realized it the first thing on hers.

As the evening progressed, Jay drank so much I wondered I how he stayed on his feet. But he still sounded lucid. "How do you like the party, Clark?"

"It's fine," I said. "Where's Jenny?"

"She's over there, decorating your tree."

Jay twisted his head around and saw Jenny stringing his tree with lights. "That's nice of her. I never would have gotten around to decorating it myself."

"Well, at least you have one," I said. Jenny and I couldn't afford one.

January 5, 1981

"I know now what I want to do, Hon. I can see my future, and it excites me," I said. We were walking side by side toward a West Salem smorgasbord. The restaurant was having a three dollar a head special this day, and Jenny and I were going there planning to eat three days' worth of food all at once. I had decided that the walk would be a good time to discuss my college plans with her. "I really think I can be almost anything I want to be, if I give myself the chance to learn and grow," I said.

"I thought you knew what you wanted to do when you married me," Jenny replied. She stopped briefly and kicked a small pebble down the sidewalk.

"I did, Plum. And I need you very much. But I also need to go to school. If you like, we can arrange things so you can go to school, too."

Jenny stopped abruptly and gave me a stare as hard as the diamond on her wedding ring. "I don't want to go to college," she said tersely.

"Okay, if that's what you want," I said. I affectionately placed my hand upon her shoulder. "But I want to go."

Jenny tore my hand off her shoulder and started walking away from me. "What's wrong?" I asked as politely as I could when I caught up with her.

"I want to settle down!" she said loudly. Her eyes were reddish, and she was on the brink of crying.

"Honey," I said while trying to keep up with increased pace of her walk, "I want to settle down, too." I paused, trying to come up with something that would quiet her down. Finally, it came to me. "Because I'm the father bird, I want to make sure that I can afford to buy enough straw to build a good nest for our chicks." This turned out to be all Jenny needed to calm down for the time being.

January 13, 1981

I went to Yamhill College to discuss the possibilities of enrolling there in the fall. It had looked picture perfect when I had visited Darrel. I figured if it were good enough for Darrel, it was good enough for me. Darrel eagerly met me when I arrived on campus. He introduced me to various deans and professors, who were all exceptionally friendly with me. Darrel made certain that I had all the forms that I needed for enrollment. The biggest problem I was going to be facing was financial. This was a private school and that meant tuition would be expensive. The only way I would be able to afford it would be to go through a lengthy process of filling out financial aid forms. However, it was something I really wanted to do, all of a sudden.

That night Jenny watched me come into the apartment carrying all the forms and pamphlets I had picked up at Yamhill. I put the materials down on the coffee table, gave her a kiss, and went to the bathroom. When I returned I noticed her picking through the college material with a certain amount of curiosity. "I think you'd like

Yamhill, Hon," I said. "It's very quiet, and it has plenty of grass and trees." Her response was to give me a weak smile, after which she told me that dinner was ready. The rest of the evening she seemed to have something that was troubling her. Every time I tried to learn what, though, she'd always say it was nothing. It wasn't until we were crawling into bed that she let me know.

"Clark?"

"Yes, Plum?"

"I don't think you should go to Yamhill."

"What do you mean you don't want me to go to Yamhill?" I asked, shocked and angry that she would offer me that sort of advice.

"I think it's all just a pipe dream. You could never get the money to go there, it's like you're living in some kind of dream."

"The people at the college said money should be no problem if I filled out the forms. I think I can do it, it's not a dream at all."

"Why don't you just go back to that place you went to before?" She asked, as she crept closer to my side of the bed.

"You mean the teacher's college?"

"I think you should go back there and prove that you can--"

"Honey--"

"Please listen. I think you should go back there and prove that you can make it there, since you didn't when you went there before."

"But, honey, I...".

"If you don't, you'll spend the rest of your life wondering why you couldn't make it there."

She had a point. State Teacher's College would not be the financial headache that Yamhill would be.

"Okay," I agreed, "I'll go back to the teacher's college." Jenny tried to put her arms around me, but I pulled away from her.

"What wrong, Clark?"

"Nothing, honey. I'm just very tired tonight," I said. I didn't say a word to her about the pain of regret rapidly forming in my gut.

Jenny's Diary

The cookies came out so well! Even though I made them! I don't make notes in this book very often, but I had to just write this down! My mom and sisters always did most of the cooking at home. They always said they didn't trust me with fire, and they would all start giggling. Maybe it was funny the first time they said, but it got really old after it became some sort of family tradition they had to say whenever we were in the kitchen. All they would trust me with making on my own were butter biscuits in the morning. And I do bake good biscuits, but there's so much more to me than that. Like chocolate chip cookies! With extra chips. I secretly bought the stuff to make them, after saving a dime here and there for some time. Clark really likes my biscuits, but wait until he tastes these cookies. I've put on the dress he likes, and it's a good thing I checked my face, because there was flour all over it. He should be home any minute, I'm excited because I know once he tries these cookies he will finally love me.

CHAPTER THIRTEEN

For a moment, it seemed as everything was going to work out well. I started going to college, with the help of all kinds of financial aid I hadn't known existed. Jenny even found a new job. Cleaning Jay's house. Three times a week Jenny would go to his house, which was five blocks from our apartment. Sometimes Jay even picked her up and often brought her home as well. I wasn't sure if I liked the idea of my dream girl being a cleaning lady. The extra dollars, however, helped reduce the growls in our stomachs. I couldn't believe how poor we were. There wasn't much left after paying the rent and electricity each month. Here I was, working in a restaurant, and still we had little to eat. We often lived on oatmeal and pancakes. For dinner. I was more convinced than ever that my plan on going to college was the right one. How else could I be qualified to earn the kind of living my wife deserved?

March 15, 1981

Finishing my shift at Rod's at four o'clock, I came home and watched TV. Jenny was working at Jay's. Lately she had seemed distant. She was upset about something. Learning what she was upset about was difficult. I had tried, but soon discovered clipping my toenails with a chain saw was easier than finding out what was bothering Jenny.

Around 6 PM, I heard the sound of Jay's pickup truck dropping Jenny off. When she walked into our apartment, she saw me and got a strange expression on her face. I couldn't tell whether it was a look of anger, a look of hate, or a look of fear. Whatever it was, it was completely aimed at me.

"I want to quit," she said. In her tone was something that made me feel as if some had tossed an ice cube down the back of my shirt.

"Why do you want to quit?" I asked.

"Because I want to settle down. It's time we started a family."

"Well, we're working on it. That's why I'm going to college."

"I don't want to go to college," Jenny screamed. Then, before I knew what was happening, something hit me in the face. Jenny had grabbed a dirty glass sitting on the couch, and had thrown it hard into my face. The glass had broken, and I was bleeding. Jenny had gone berserk, and was screaming while she threw things on the floor. Taking refuge in the bathroom, I locked the door and quickly checked my face in the mirror. Though it was bloody, it was just a little scratch. I washed my face off in the sink, while trying not to hear the sound of Jenny throwing things around. Finally, things sounded quiet. Putting my ear up to the bathroom door, all I could hear now were the sounds of Jenny crying. After putting a bandage on my face, I slowly opened the door and came out. The living room was a mess. Right in the middle of it sat Jenny, crying like a little girl. She looked up at me, and looked sadder than anybody I'd ever seen. "Please take care of me," she sobbed.

"What do you mean, Jenny?"

"I just need somebody to take care of me."

"How?"

"Could you hold me?"

I sat on the floor next to her, and pulled my dream girl into my arms. Soon she crawled into my lap, and I rocked her back and forth as she quietly sobbed, until she fell asleep. Then, carrying her into our bedroom, I pulled her shoes off and put her into bed. Then I went back to the living room and started picking things up, trying not to start crying myself.

The next morning Jenny seemed normal again. She acted embarrassed over what had happened the day before. We spent the day quietly reading the Sunday paper and watching television together. A standard day together for us. We usually spent more time looking at the television than we did the beauty that existed in each of us. At 4:30, I went into the bedroom and came back dressed in my Rod's uniform. "Where do you think you're going?" Jenny asked.

"To work."

"Why?"

"One of us has to, and since you're not going to work for Jay anymore, it has to be me."

Jenny sprang from where she was sitting on the couch and marched to where I was standing near the door. "I never want you to go to Rod's ever again," she said, with an unnatural look on her face that could spook a horse.

"Why not?" I asked, not having the slightest guess why my wife was acting this way.

"You know why not, you pinhead."

"No, I don't, Please tell me."

"You're in love with one of the girls at Rod's."

"Don't be ridiculous, honey, you know that you're the one girl I wanted, out of all the ones who work at the place. After all, I did marry you."

"Why did you marry me?"

"Because I'm in love with you."

"No, you're not."

"Honey, I really need to go to work," I said. "The reason I'm going is because we need the money. That's the only reason."

"We don't need the money, we can go live with your parents. We could all be one big happy family."

I could not believe what I was hearing. After finally getting out on my own, here she was wanting me to go back home. "I don't want to live with my folks."

"Well, tough, because that's what we're going to do."

"I'm going to work," I said, as I moved toward the door.

Before I moved very far, though, Jenny's open hand smashed against my face. To keep her from doing it again, I grabbed her by her wrists, but she managed to pull them free. She then ran to the kitchen and returned seconds later with a long slicing knife, which she put up to her throat. "What are you doing?" I asked, shocked.

"Either you call Rod's and tell them you're not coming in tonight, or I'll kill myself."

I wasn't about to call Jenny's bluff. Judging from the way she was acting, she was likely to do anything.

"Rod's West," Denna answered.

"This is Clark. I'm afraid I won't be able to come in tonight," I said, keeping my unblinking eyes trained on Jenny and her knife.

"Are you serious, Clark?" Denna asked. "You're supposed to be here in ten minutes."

"Yes, Denna, I'm very serious."

"Jay will have to fire you for this, if you go ahead and do it."

"I'm afraid that's what he'll have to do then."

"Okay," Denna said sadly. "I'll miss you, friend." Denna hung up the phone, and I stood holding my phone receiver in my hand, with my eyes still on Jenny. I lowered the phone until it was resting on the floor, and she did the same with the knife. Then, for a reason I'll never totally understand, I went to her and held her in my arms gently.

A few minutes later the phone rang. "Clark, what's going on?" Jay asked, after I had answered.

"Jenny didn't want me to go to work tonight."

"That's the only reason you're not coming in?"

"Well," I said. I checked to see that Jenny was out of hearing distance as she prepared dinner in the kitchen. "Jenny said she would use the knife she was holding up to her throat if I went ahead and reported to work."

"She's that much against you working for us?"

"I guess so."

"Well, without you to manage the
shift, we're going to have to close the
store in an hour. It's too late to find
someone else in the chain to sub for
you. Everyone else at our own place
has already worked as many hours as
they can this week. What do you consider more important, your marriage
or your restaurant career?"

"I guess my marriage," I said,
though it was a very tough choice at
that moment.

"Don't do it, Clark. You can always
find another woman. And take it from
me, Jenny's not worth it. I know, I've
been there twice myself. Dump her.
Dump her right now."

"I can't do that," I said.

"Then I'm really going to miss
you," Jay said.

"I'll miss you, Jay."

"Well, fine, if that's what you want."
Just like that, Jay hung up.

Jenny started crying. I wasn't in the
mood to comfort her. I glumly spent
the rest of the night being silent, despite Jenny's efforts to make up for her
behavior.

Jenny returned to her quiet and sweet self after that night. And why not, I thought. She had gotten what she wanted that night. I continued going to college without any problems, at least that I knew about. Our finances, though, were full of problems. We had our rent, the car payments, and everything else to pay. Our savings could only last us two months, and not much more even if we were careful. Since I was a full-time student, I decided to get a student loan. I worked out the arrangements and filled out the forms. Finally only one thing needed to be done, and that was for Jenny to sign them. I did not think this would be much of a problem, since she had been very passive of late. But I was wrong.

"I won't sign it," Jenny said, after I had approached her with pen and ink as she was loading dishes into the dishwasher.

"Why not, Plum?" I asked, trying to keep our discussion light.

"Because I don't feel like going into debt."

"Well, if that's the way you feel, why'd you manage to get both of us unemployed so fast?" I wasn't attempting lightness anymore.

"You don't want me anymore, do you?" Jenny asked.

The tightness of her pupils was matched by the grip she had on the coffee mug she was holding.

"Well, after the way you got me fired, I have to admit that I've been thinking it over."

Jenny's eyes now blazed, and she sent the coffee mug flying toward my head. It missed, smashing into pieces against the wall behind me, Jenny ran past me, and I turned and followed. She started throwing my belongings out the front door. I tried to stop her, but before I got anywhere something slammed against my face. When I awoke, I was lying face down in a small puddle of blood. I could hear Jenny calling the police on the phone. Near my head I saw the object that had struck me--my psychology textbook. I got back to my feet and waited for the dizziness to subside. I checked my nose to make certain it wasn't bleeding be-cause it was broken, and made my way into the living room. Then I saw the glass. It was scattered over everything, and it had come from the large picture window in the center of the living room. Jenny, in her rage, had thrown something through it. She stood near the window, with fear in her eyes.

"I've called the police for you," she said meekly. "What have I done, Clark? Why did I do this?"

"I don't know. It looks like the police have arrived." We could both look out the broken window and see the police car as it parked. A lone officer emerged from the vehicle and in seconds was knocking on our door.

"Well, it looks like you've been having a disagreement here," the officer said after we had let him in. "Who's responsible for all this damage?"

"I am, sir." Jenny responded.

"And you bloodied up his face?" he asked, pointing to me.

"Yes," Jenny said, staring down at her feet.

"What'd he do to make you so angry?"

"Nothing. I just got mad."

"Oh. My name is Lew Krasnik," he said, walking to me and putting his hand warmly on my shoulder.

"I'm Clark Jackson, and this is my wife, Jenny," I said, as he scribbled our names down on his pad. We took turns describing what happened, with him sitting on the couch between us, taking notes. He was in his thirties, of average height and medium build. His hair was of a blend between the colors of red and blonde, and he had a full mustache. He seemed sincerely concerned about what had happened between us.

"I think you should press charges," he finally said, looking at me. He drew a box on his notepad and wrote something inside it. "Sign this down at the bottom, and I'll take her in," he said, holding his pen and pad out to me. Jenny's eyes grew large as I took the pad and pen. For a moment, I saw my dream girl again.

"I can't do this," I said, giving Officer Krasnik back his pen and pad. Jenny smiled in relief.

"You're getting off very easy, girl," Krasnik said to Jenny. "I want you both to promise to get some sort of counseling. If you can't afford it, there is a police program you can go to."

"That's okay," I responded. "They have a counseling program at my college."

"And you two are responsible for replacing the broken window, understand?"

"Yes;" Jenny and I said in unison.

"I'm going to leave now, but I think it would be best if you two separated for a little while, just to let things cool down a little. Does either of you have another place to go spend the night at?"

"I guess I could go out to my parents' place," I said.

"Great," the officer said. After he left, I rapidly threw some things into our car. Some were the possessions Jenny had thrown out, because I was afraid of what she might do to them after I left. The whole time I was doing this, she sat sadly on the couch, watching and crying.

Jenny's Diary

Clark spends so much time at school. At least, that's what he tells me. I don't believe it. He probably has another girl. Just like he did at Rod's. I don't know why he married me. He doesn't want to settle down. He just wants to play. With other girls. By being in college. Isn't going to school what kids do? We need to settle down. I dream of the day he will come home from work and play catch with our son. But at this rate, it's never going to happen, and I just want to scream!

CHAPTER FOURTEEN

Clark Jackson's Journal

My parents heard about the fight, and how our money situation had gone from hopeless too impossible because of the cost of replacing the broken window. They insisted we move in with them. I felt like such a failure. I didn't want to leave our dream apartment, but our bills had become a nightmare. I hoped Jenny would behave herself better if my mom was always around.

October 31, 1981

The day finally came when my father's Chevy pickup came to move us back home. Most of our belongings were stacked in my parents' garage, since there was no room for them inside the house. We visited our dream apartment one last time, leaving our keys inside when we locked the door and left for my parents' home. "Oh, by the way, happy anniversary," I said, a day late.

November 15, 1981

At 2:30, I drove up in front of my parents' home, after having been at school. Jenny was waiting to greet me as I got out of the car, and we gave each other a light kiss. Then I sprang the big new I had upon her, "Guess what, Plum?"

"What, Clark?"

"We have a place to live."

"I know we do, here with your folks."

"I mean a place of our own, again."

A stern look grew on Jenny's face. "How are we supposed to pay for it?"

"It's a great big house, and we're not going to have to pay any rent for it at all."

"Why's that?"

"A professor died at an East Coast school."

"So?"

"So they asked one of the professors at the Teacher's College to fill, in for the guy for the rest of the year, and this Prof needed someone to house-sit his home. I answered the ad, and now we've got the place."

"There's other things we need to pay for as well as rent."

"That'll be no problem, because my student loan came through."

"What student loan?" Jenny asked, with her pupils now the size of pencil tips.

"The one Dad cosigned with me on."

Jenny's mouth now started quivering, a sign that she was absolutely furious. She turned and ran into the garage. Since the garage had a door that led to the inside of the house, I figured that she had simply taken that route to get to our bedroom. I turned and started back to the car to retrieve my textbooks. I sensed something behind me and turned around just in time to duck from a metal garden hoe Jenny had swung at my head. There wasn't any doubt that Jenny had intended to hurt me with the hoe.

My mother came out of the house as Jenny swung the hoe, seeing the whole thing. "Jenny, stop acting like a baby!" she yelled, this of course only making Jenny angrier. Jenny pulled the hoe back over her head, and was about to strike the windshield of the Volkswagen with it when I grabbed the hoe and managed to pull it out of her hands and threw it over on the lawn. "Okay, this does it," my mother said. "If you two want to fight, you'll have to do it in your own home, and not mine. I want the two of you to move out of here as soon as possible." When she saw that Jenny wasn't looking, Mom gave me a quick wink, after which she dramatically marched back into the house.

"I'm sorry, Clark," said a now sympathetic Jenny.

"It now looks like we have no choice but to move into that house."

"I'm not."

"What do you mean? Where else are you going to live?"

"I'm going to stay here," she responded, while her eyes were twitching nervously back and forth.

"You heard mom, she wants both of us to get out."

"She'll forgive me."

"What about me? I am her son, you know."

"She'll forgive you, too."

I felt Jenny and I needed to be on our own if we were to make it together.

This was the only way Jenny could learn to be responsible for herself. I also knew that the crowded living arrangement was driving not only us but my entire family insane. "Well, you can stay here if you like, but I'm moving out tomorrow."

Jenny's eyes became fluorescent. "Do you mean it? I can stay here by myself?"

"You can do whatever you want," I angrily replied. I walked off alone to find a spot I knew of at the river bottom. A spot where I would be free to express the pain I was feeling, the pain of now knowing that Jenny had never wanted me. She had only wanted my family home.

When I returned, my mother was waiting for me outside the house. "I hope you aren't too mad at the way I spoke earlier, son" she said. "I was just trying to be so sinister that Jenny would want to turn against me, instead of you. Just remember, until this thing cools down, I'll be the bad guy."

"Okay, Mom."

"What's happening, anyway?"

"Well, I have this house we can live in rent free, and I'm moving there tomorrow."

"What about your wife?"

"She insists that she's going to stay here."

"Oh," Mom said, not mentioning anything else.

Even though Jenny and I weren't talking to each other, we did sleep in the same bed that night. However, we were as far apart as it is possible to be on a full-sized mattress.

The next morning, I awoke early and quickly set about throwing the things together that I would need right away in the new house. Jenny got out of bed as soon as I did, and watched me as I took my possessions out to the Volkswagen.

"Did you remember your typewriter?" she asked, sweetly.

"Yes, I did," I replied gruffly, even though I was pleased that she had mentioned it.

"What are you looking for, honey?" she asked, as I was looking through our closet.

"What happened to our towels?"

"Here, take this one," she said. She handed me a white towel, which I didn't notice until much later was monogrammed "his."

"Thanks," I said, stuffing the towel into my backpack.

Without another word I was out the door, in the Volkswagen, and off to both school and my new home.

I went to my morning classes on schedule, and the day was running along very smoothly. For a day in mid-November, the weather was surprisingly mild. As I walked out onto a sidewalk after getting out of my 11:00 to 12:00 class, I tried to catch the entire sun in my face. My enjoyment was interrupted by a shove from behind. It was Jenny, and her mouth was quivering.

"What are you doing here?" I asked.

"I'm here to get my husband!" she tensely said.

"Did Mom bring you?"

"No. She hates me."

"Then how did you get here?"

"I walked."

It was fifteen miles from my parents' farm to the college. I knew that whatever Jenny wanted from me was of a serious nature. "Can we go to the College Center to talk, so we'll be out of the sun?" I asked. I thought Jenny would be less likely to have an emotional outburst in a very public place.

"I don't want to go anywhere at this stupid place," Jenny said. She suddenly slammed her closed fist into my unprotected mouth, in the process splitting open my bottom lip.

"All I want to do is talk with you!" I said through my sore mouth.

"Okay," Jenny said. We went to the center and sat on an unoccupied sofa.

"What happened at home?" I asked.

"Don't you know? Your mother told me she didn't want me living there."

"Did she tell you why?"

"I didn't wait around for her explanations. I just walked straight out the door."

"And you walked here." "Yeah."

"What do you want, Jenny?"

"I want you!" She reached out and pulled my glasses off my face, threatening through her motions to destroy them if I tried to pull anything funny on her. "I want a farm, I want to have a baby, I want to be a housewife."

"But Jenny, how can we afford those things? We don't even have jobs. I mean, it costs money to own and operate a farm."

"If you can get a loan to go to school with, you can get a loan to buy a farm with."

"But that's not the same thing."

"Either you come away with me now, or you're going to be sorry."

"How am I going to be sorry?"

"You'll never get rid of me. Wherever you go, I'll be right behind you."

"There are ways I can keep you from doing that," I said, thinking in particular about the police.

"I'd like to see you try."

By this point, my only concern was for my safety, and I decided to take Jenny up on her dare. Through my nearsighted eyes, I could see the campus information desk fifty yards away. I decided to try to make it to the desk and ask for the police. I hoped the ugly creature beside me would not try to kill me in the process. I rose from the sofa and slowly walked to the info desk. Jenny followed closely, clutching my glasses firmly.

"Clark, I want you to stop all of this foolishness about college. You don't see what you're doing. You're using people."

By this time, we had reached the desk. I quickly asked the woman manning the desk if I could use the phone. "I'm sorry, but you'll have to use a pay phone, unless this is an emergency," the woman said.

"This is an emergency," I said.

"What is the nature of this emergency?" the lady asked.

I looked at Jenny, who tightened her grip on my glasses. "I want to call the police," I announced loudly.

"NO!" Jenny screamed at the top of her lungs, and as she did she broke up my glasses and sent them flying all over the large room. Her fists then started plowing into me. I didn't fight back. Instead, I just stood there and let her hit me, since no degree of physical abuse could match the grief in my heart. A large crowd of people quickly gathered around us.

"What's she doing to him?" asked a female student rather loudly. By this time, I was crouched on the floor with Jenny still firing away with her fists on top of me. Finally, a little gray-haired lady came in and tore Jenny off me.

"Arrest her!" I screamed, while pointing aggressively at Jenny.

We were taken to separate rooms in the College Center to wait for the police to arrive. About fifteen minutes later, a campus security guard came into the room where I was.

"Do you think you could talk your wife into going with us to the security building? She doesn't seem to trust me," the guard said.

Jenny was brought in, and she became glued to my side as we walked to the other building. "A county sheriff has been called. He'll meet us at the security building," the guard said.

We went inside the small building and were seated at a long table in what appeared to be the main room. After we quietly waited for a couple of minutes, the police officer arrived. It was Lew Krasnik. "I thought I told you to stop cutting this guy up," he yelled at Jenny. Seeing my bloody mouth, he made a face. He then went with me to a different room, where I told him my version of the story. Jenny gave her side to the security guard in the other room. "I would press charges this time, if I were you," Krasnik said as we went back to the long table in the other room. The two officers conferred in another part of the room for a few minutes. "Your stories match," Krasnik said. Jenny was passive again, not holding anything back which could get her in trouble. I now felt that this honesty was just her way of making me not feel like pressing charges against her. "Do you wish to press charges?" Officer Krasnik asked me. All the eyes in the room were of course focused on me.

"This time, yes," I said.

"What?" Jenny asked, with a bit of confusion. "That's not fair. He's as guilty as I am!" The niceness was now totally gone from Jenny.

"He didn't get violent," Officer Krasnik snapped, pointing a finger at Jenny. "You're going to have to learn you can't get away with behavior like this."

"Jackson, you're a jerk!" Jenny yelled, as the security guard removed her from the room.

"This is the best thing you can do," Krasnik said, after Jenny was gone. "She can now be forced by the court to seek some help for her problems."

"Yeah, but my marriage is over."

"You're not the only person in the world with that problem," Krasnik said, as he pulled some papers from his briefcase for me to sign. We had finished the paperwork, and were discussing what was going to happen, when the security guard came back into the room.

"She would like to see her husband once more before she goes to lockup."

Krasnik looked at me sympathetically. "You don't have to see her if you don't want to."

"I do want to see her again," I answered. They took me into the next room where Jenny was seated in a wooden chair with her hands behind her back. Her head was hanging down, and she didn't seem to notice that I was there. "I'm sorry, Jenny," I said softly. "I don't want to do this to you, but I have little choice." I wanted to tell her that I still loved her. The guard and Krasnik were standing directly behind me, though, and I felt too inhibited. I took a long look at Jenny, who was still totally ignoring me, and found that I couldn't think of anything else to say to her.

"Are you through?" the guard asked.

"Yes, I guess I am," I said.

Krasnik told the guard that he would take Jenny to a Salem area jail, and motioned for her to stand. Only then did I notice that she was handcuffed. Just as in the movies. Krasnik led her outside. I followed, watching Jenny take the long march to the patrol car. Then, right before she sat in the backseat of the car, she underwent a transformation before my eyes. Suddenly, she was no longer the ugly creature who had attacked me. Instead, she was my dream girl with the sad blue eyes again. I wanted to scream at Krasnik to let her go, so she could be safe in my arms. I was supposed to protect my wife, not have the cops take her away in chains. However, I couldn't move. I couldn't speak. I couldn't even wipe the tears from my eyes as the woman I thought would always be at my side was carried away by the patrol car, taking my heart with her.

CHAPTER FIFTEEN

November 19, 1981

"Hello, Darrel," I said.

"Enter," Darrel said, motioning for me to come into his apartment. "Where's...?"

"Jenny?"

"Yes."

"It's a little hard to explain," I said.

"Gone?"

Yes."

"Forever?"

"I think so."

"Upset?"

"Of course I'm upset. What do you think I am, Darrel?"

"Lost."

"You bet I am." Darrel wasn't necessarily the most understanding person, but right now he was all I had. So I let go of the thoughts that were tearing-my heart apart. "I just don't understand what happened with Jenny. I love her more than anything. I don't know what she is so scared of. I mean, I only tried to give her what we all quietly scream for...".

"Clark, you know what your problem is?"

"What?"

"You care too much."

December, 1981

I continued my classes as if nothing had happened. I went to all my classes, and did all my work. I crossed my t's and dotted my i's. But I was uncomfortable looking at my eyes and face in a mirror. The large house I was living in rent free seemed so empty even my unspoken thoughts seemed to echo when I was alone. But even thought I had plenty of time to think, thinking was the one thing I couldn't do. Jenny was gone. Gone forever, for all I knew. The same day I had her led off in handcuffs, the police let her go on her own recognizance, and Jenny went back to Washington. She missed her court appearance. To make me feel better Officer Krasnik told me if she ever set foot in Oregon again she'd be in big trouble. But I told him to forget it, to drop the charges. Putting Jenny behind bars wouldn't make my heart feel any better.

January 6, 1982

"She's here," my mother said over the phone.

"Jenny?" I asked, not believing what I was hearing.

"Yes," my mother continued, using a heavy whisper.

"She's here, with her whole family. And a truck."

"A truck?"

"Yes, and they're loading up all the things you guys stored in the garage. You want me to call the police?"

"No. I'll be right over." I ran out to the Volkswagen, and raced to my parents' place. I didn't want to stop Jenny. She could take everything. I wanted to at least say good-bye. Pulling into my parents' driveway, however, I could see that I was too late. There wasn't a truck in sight.

"I tried to keep them here, but they left five minutes ago," my mother said.

We walked into the garage, and I saw that it was now almost totally empty. Everything was missing, even things I'd owned long before meeting Jenny. Even things belonging to my parents. There was only one thing left on the bare cement floor. "What's that?" I asked my mother.

"I don't know," my mother said.

Walking to the black object, I saw that it was a book. Picking it up, I discovered it was a Bible. The book was open, and my eyes landed on the page I knew she meant for me to see:

"To everything there is a season, and a time to every purpose under the heaven:

A time to be born, and a time to die; a time to plant, and a time to pluck up that which is planted;

A time to kill, and a time to heal; a time to break down, and a time to build up;

A time to weep, and a time to laugh; a time to mourn, and a time to dance;

A time to cast away stones, and a time to gather stones together; a time to embrace, and a time to refrain from embracing;

A time to get, and a time to lose; a time to keep, and a time to cast away;

A time to rend, and a time to sew; a time to keep silence, and a time to speak;

A time to love, and a time to hate; a time of war, and a time of peace."

I didn't feel better. And I didn't even know if I understood better.

January 9, 1982

"There," my father said, as he tightened the nut on the new fender he'd put on my Volkswagen. "Now your car's in one piece again."

"It looks good," I said.

"You know," my father said, leaning his hand on my shoulder. "It's funny, really."

"What is?"

"Just that you've driven this car so long with that crushed fender. You probably thought it would never be fixed. And just like that, in a few minutes, it's like the whole thing never happened. I think there's a lesson in that somewhere. "

"What kind of lesson?" I now knew why, after so long, my father had finally made time to fix my fender. My father rarely tried to advise me, so I went along and tried to enjoy it.

"Well, sometimes we have things go wrong in life."

"You mean, instead of crushed fenders, we have crushed feelings."

"Exactly. And you'll go everywhere with these crushed feelings, thinking they'll always be with you."

"And then, one day, right out of the blue, my dad will call me up. And just like that, my feelings won't be crushed anymore."

My father sighed. "Okay, so I'd be a terrible television father. In fact, I've been feeling like I wasn't that great of real dad to you."

It was the craziest thing. As I stood there, looking at my father, a man I had thought I'd known all my life, I realized something I'd never noticed before. He wasn't just a face. He was a man. A man with feelings. "I wouldn't say that, Dad."

"I feel like what happened with Jenny was my fault. If I'd been there more for you, taught you more, maybe it all would have turned out better."

"Look, Dad, you did just fine."

"But I really should have spent more time with you." "You were the best dad you could be. And besides, it's all in the past now. You can't do anything about it now, but try to be better in the future."

"Say, you don't happen to think that same advice would apply to a guy who tried to be a perfect husband, but fell short? Or do you think a guy like that should spend the rest of his life never forgiving himself?"

After saying good-bye to my Dad, I drove off in my repaired Volkswagen. I thought about what my Dad said, and I guess he had a point. But I knew I was at least partly to blame for what happened. As I've tried to put all the pieces back together of our time together, I've realized something horrible. I knew that I was never going to see Jenny again.

But I now know that I had never really seen Jenny at all. My picture of Jenny, how I wanted to see her, had little to do with what she was really like.

Driving around a corner, a deer appeared directly in my path. But now I drive much slower than I used to, and was able to stop without hitting it.

CHAPTER SIXTEEN

February 27, 1990

I could tell by the excitement in her voice that Wendy had something important to tell me. "Are you sitting down?" she asked.

I gripped the phone tight. "The detective?" I asked.

"Yes. Do you want to know where Jenny is living?"

"He found her?"

"Yes."

I had been standing, but I took my second wife's advice and sat. Though I still thought of Jenny a lot, I'd long before let go all hope of ever finding out what ever happened to her. "Where is she?" I asked quietly.

"Hold on. She lives about a mile from us. She's married, and her name is Medily. She had two children, a boy and a girl." A great sense of relief came over me. It sounded as if Jenny had achieved her dreams. "Are you okay?"

"Yes," I answered, quietly.

"The detective left a couple of sheets of information for us to look over."

I was glad I had only one class left before the end of the day, and nothing planned after it. I don't know if my students saw how edgy I was. As soon as the class was over, I raced out of the high school faster than most of the students.

"This is all we get for two hundred dollars?" I asked, as Wendy showed me the thin packet the private detective had given us.

"It says enough," Wendy said, handing the sheets to me. There it was, in black and white.

"Isn't that something," I said softly. "All this time, I've wondered about her, and where she was. And it turns out she's only five minutes away."

"Do you want to go see her?"

"No. It'd just be awkward and em- barrassing. I mean, I've grown up so much since then. And I can only hope she has too. We would be like total strangers."

"I think you need to see with your own eyes that she's okay. You don't have to meet her. We could just park across the street, and wait in the car to catch a glimpse of her."

I looked at my sweet, beautiful wife. For a girl who grew up on a dairy farm, she could come up with the sneakiest ideas. "You mean, like we were a couple of cops on stakeout, or something?"

"Yeah. Let's have some fun."

"No. It's good enough just knowing she's okay."

"Are we still heading out for pizza tonight?"

"Sure. Let me go change first."

Going into the bedroom, I changed out of my teaching clothes. Then, unable to resist the temptation, I pulled out from my bottom dresser drawer a small photograph book. About a year after I had last seen Jenny, my mother got around to developing a box full of film. She discovered that several of the rolls were of my wedding with Jenny. For several years, I tormented myself by looking at them. But since marrying Wendy two years earlier, I hadn't looked at them once until now. There was Darrel, looking uncomfortable over the whole affair. I wondered how he was doing. Strange how even the closest friendships from high school can just fade away, almost without a person noticing.

Denna was in the pictures, too, crying harder than anyone else. I wondered how all the folks at Rod's were doing now. I'd stopped by there the year before with Wendy, but none of the old gang worked there anymore. Hadn't in years. Not even Jay. I didn't even recognize the place anymore. A former professional basketball player owned it now, and had totally remodeled the joint, to make more room for his sports awards.

And there was my dream girl. I had changed a great deal. In these pictures, though, Jenny was just as I would always remember her best. A frail, pretty little girl with blond curls and piercing blue eyes begging for someone to love them. And that I had, and still did. Many people, meaning to give comfort, had suggested that what I had with Jenny wasn't really a marriage. It was just an affair, a fling, and our only mistake was making it legal. But they were wrong. I was right in thinking my love for Jenny was real. But I was wrong in thinking I was ready to be a husband.

And Jenny wasn't ready to be a wife. A committed relationship built on the foundations of happiness requires grownups. Looking at the pictures now, I still can't believe how much I look like a child in them.

"Caught you," Wendy said, coming into the bedroom and sitting next to me on the bed. "Come on, honey. I know you're dying of curiosity."

"But it seems so childish, playing spies."

"Your mind won't be at ease until you see for yourself that she's okay. We once had this cow on the farm."

"Not another farm story."

"You know you enjoy my farm stories. Anyway, there was this cow who had a calf. And, of course, on a dairy the mothers are quickly separated from their calves, and usually for a day or two the mothers will bawl for their calves. And this cow was no different. But this cow was my favorite. She had quite a personality for a cow. And I felt sorry for her. So I opened the door to where the calf was being kept, and let the mother cow see her. And this cow was bright for a cow. She knew her calf couldn't be with her. She just wanted to know her calf was okay. All she did was stick her head through the door, see that her baby was okay, and then walk back to the hay trough. And she never bellowed for her baby again. It was if she understood why they had to be separated, but she needed to see her one more time, just to be sure everything was okay."

"Sounds like the Einstein of cows."

"That's why she was my favorite."

I looked at my wife's sweet smile. Wendy was the best thing that had ever happened to me. "You know, I'm not from the big city either, but I've never been one to give human personalities to farm animals."

"I couldn't help it. They were so cute, and I was twelve."

"I think you're cute," I said, kissing her.

"How about it? Just a quick look so you'll know she's okay? I think it would help you sleep better from now on."

Wendy knew me well. "Why not?" I said.

All while we drove the short distance to where Jenny was supposed to live, Wendy tried to keep me preoccupied with talk about things she was doing at church. I listened, heard every syllable, but couldn't stop wondering about Jenny. I guess it was selfish, but I wondered whether I'd ever mattered to her the way she had mattered to me.

Halfway there, the Oregon skies broke loose with rivers of rain. And I'm not exaggerating. The visibility was zero, but I continued driving. When we reached the street Jenny was supposed to live on, I slowed down so we wouldn't miss her address. As the rain continued to pour, we drove up and down the street without success.

"What was the house number again?" I asked, pulling the car into an empty lot.

"3005."

"Well, that house across the street is 3004, and the one up ahead is 3006. I may be crazy, but I think this empty lot is 3005."

"There's one way to find out," Wendy said, unbuckling her seat belt and opening the door.

"Where are you going?"

"Just call me Wendy Jackson, girl detective." Wendy took off running across the street to the house marked 3004, leaving me little choice but to follow.

"Excuse me," Wendy said to the older lady who opened the door.

"We're looking for Jenny Medily and her family."

"Come on inside," the lady said, "before the rain washes you two away."

"I don't know about this," I whispered, as we waited in the front doorway for the lady to return with some towels.

"We're not doing anything wrong," Wendy said, smiling.

The lady brought the towels, and after we dried off, the lady showed us to her living room. "So you're friends of the Medily's," she said.

"Yes," Wendy said. "My husband is."

"I know Jenny," I said awkwardly. "She's not expecting us."

"We, we were just in the area, and decided to drop by for a visit," Wendy added.

"I'm surprised Jenny didn't let you know she moved," the lady said.

"Well...", I stammered. "It's been some time since I've seen her, and this was the last address we had for her."

"I'm sorry to say the Medily's moved up to Longview several months ago," the lady said. "And their house was torn down. It had a bad foundation. But, for the time being, Jenny's garden is still there. That lady really loved that garden. She spent hours on it. I go over to water it from time to time. Tonight, of course, it's not necessary."

"So you knew Jenny well," Wendy said.

"Such a dear girl. Shy, but sweet. And such beautiful children. Let me show you."

The lady showed us pictures of Jenny, looking about the same as I remembered her. The pictures included her new husband, a friendly looking guy. And her two children. The boy was stocky like his dad, and the girl tiny, blond, and fragile like her mom. I thought about how these might have been my children. Wendy and I hadn't started our family yet, and Jenny was already a parent twice. In all the pictures, Jenny looked much happier than I had ever seen her. It bothered me that I could never have put that smile on her face.

"Thanks for everything," I said, as we walked to the door to leave.

"Good, it looks like the rain has finally stopped," the lady said, opening the door for us. "Now you can take a good look at Jenny's garden. That should take care of any questions you have left, Clark."

Wendy looked frozen. And I guess I must have too. "How did you know my name?" I asked.

"Jenny still had pictures of you."

"I'm glad she wasn't mad," Wendy said as we walked back to the vacant lot.

"Yeah," I said. We got back into the car. I started it, turned on the headlights, and could see the garden now that the air wasn't full of rain. The lady was right. I had my answer. The small garden only grew African Violets.

Jane Comer